"Sin Eater—a person who, through ritual means, would take on, by the act of eating food and drink over the body of a deceased corpse, the sins of that person, thus absolving the soul and allowing the person to rest in peace."

"Vengeance—punishment inflicted in retaliation for an injury or offense."

Merriam Webster

Passion
for
Vengeance

Passion
for
Vengeance

PATTY G. HENDERSON

BLANCA ROSA Publishing

2013

PASSION FOR VENGEANCE

Book Cover: Boulevard Photografica/Patty G. Henderson
www.boulevardphotografica.yolasite.com

A Short Thank You....

I could not let the opportunity go by without taking the moment to thank two very special friends who had a big part in making PASSION FOR VENGEANCE a reality. Claudia McCants and Tarra Thomas, thank you for the support and enthusiasm for my writing and for your hard work on this book in particular. Without your diligence and reading skills, PASSION FOR VENGEANCE would not have been the book it became.

And as always, my mama, Blanche Rose, who still lives and breathes in each and every book I write. I love you forever.

Patty G. Henderson
February, 2013

For Tarra

Chapter 1

*P*eter Porter was a lawyer. Facts and figures were what he dealt with. He was not prone to hasty decisions or flights of fantasy. But the woman who stood before him was truly remarkable. He had never been blessed with seeing such a woman in his life before.

"Please, have a seat Miss Emma Stiles," Porter said in his gruff business voice. All his friends knew he was a gentle soul beneath the rough voice. "I'm afraid that with the wagons going by all day, dust is difficult at most to control here." He cast his gaze away from her and around his cluttered office.

"I am no stranger to country life, Mr. Porter. It is nothing, really," the woman said in a low, even voice.

She sat down in the chair across from his big, scarred wood desk. As a chair, it was a nice one, reserved for clients only. But Porter, even in his limited fantasies, never imagined such an exquisite woman would grace that chair.

Emma Stiles was tall and slender with an air of aristocracy about her. It surrounded not only her bearing, but her oval, lean face with piercing blue eyes, even nose and full Italianate mouth. Her hair, pulled back and pinned up, was as black as the wings of a raven. Atop her head sat an exquisite, wide brim hat, dipped nearly over

1

her eyes, piled high with feathers, big roses and netting. She had to have paid a pretty penny for that. But her dress told a story of more moderate means. Peter Porter's old, shrewd eyes ascertained that his stunning visitor was of modest background. The condition of her garments sadly attested to continued washings and ironing. It was obvious to knowing eyes that Emma Stiles was far from a comfortable or aristocratic place in life.

"Well, Miss Stiles, what can I help you with this fine morning?"

Miss Stiles smiled. "I am here in search of employment, Mr. Porter. It is my interest to settle here in Havens Falls. I arrived only this morning on the train from New York. I am sure you must wonder how I came to you directly, but the lady at Wilkins House inferred that you were the proper gentleman to seek if one were to need advice of any kind." Miss Stiles paused, eyeing him.

Porter nodded. "Yes, that would be Mrs. Wilkins." He laughed. "I believe she thinks me like the owl that sits in the elm tree outside her garden. Go on, Miss Stiles."

"I am in a situation where I need employment. I am orphaned, you see, Mr. Porter, and unmarried. I lost my parents years ago. Since then, I have been fending for myself, earning my way as best a woman can." She placed her gloved hands together on her lap. "I have had proper schooling and am more than proficient in sewing, cooking and any domestic job necessary to run a house. To which, I might add, I also speak two languages in addition to English and have done secretarial work for a lawyer in New York. I was now hoping to find employment as a governess or tutor, should you know of a need for one here in Havens Falls. Do you think..."

She paused, gazing at Porter. He realized he'd been staring at her.

"Well, if this doesn't beat the devil, Miss Stiles. It certainly does!" His mouth was open in surprise.

"Why do you say such? Is my request so unheard of in these parts"

He chuckled loudly. "Oh, no, miss, not at all. To the contrary, let me show you why I've reacted such." He spun in his swivel chair and pulled open a drawer. With a florid motion, he pulled out a long newspaper tear sheet, and extended it across to Miss Stiles. "I will never question the ways of Providence," he said, grinning.

Miss Stiles gave him a puzzled look as she gently took the paper from his hand and stretched it out in front of her between her gloved hands. She smiled in comprehension as she read the notice that had been heavily penciled in red:

Live in governess wanted. Must possess highest qualifications and references. Satisfying advantages for the proper party. Please apply by mail to Mr. Peter Porter, Box 920, Havens Fall, Pennsylvania.

She gazed up at Porter, her brows furrowed in question. "I'm afraid I don't understand—"

He shook his head and smiled wide, pointing at the paper she held.

"My dear Miss Stiles, what you hold there is a proof for an advertisement that has been running in New York, Philadelphia and Boston newspapers for nearly two weeks now. I had no expectations of filling the position with any of the ladies here in Havens Falls. What is even more ironic is that I received not one single response for my five dollars—that is the cost of the ad. And now—like magic, here you sit, just when I was at my rope's end. I truly did not know what avenue to turn to next until you walked in my door."

3

Miss Stiles smiled at him, yet the vivid blue of her eyes seemed incapable of reflecting the smile.

"Then, does that mean—"

"Indeed it does, Miss Stiles," Porter said with a flourish of enthusiasm. He could not control himself from taking in her stunning appearance. "I do hope you have the proper references so that we might be able to settle the matter right now."

"But surely, Mr. Porter, I would hope to have more details about your advertisement."

Porter sat back and formed a triangle with his hands. "But of course. All the details will be explained in depth but I assure you, you will not be needing your room at Mrs. Wilkins's any further. Not after you hear me out." He paused. "Have you heard of the Havens of Pennsylvania? The founders of Havens Falls?"

Emma Stiles shook her head. "I'm afraid I have not."

Porter chuckled again. "The Havens are only the most famous name in these hills. Colonel Vincent Havens was second in command to General McKenzie of the 401st Cavalry Pennsylvania and made quite a name for himself at Gettysburg. They still honor Colonel Havens hereabouts. Eleven years ago, he returned a hero. Alas, he passed away years back. He left his legacy, Havenswood, a large plantation about three miles from town. Most people swear it looks like it should belong somewhere in the South, but no, the Colonel was Union through and through. And a born farmer. He had a farmer's hand all right, turning out record crops on the Havenswood land..." He paused and fiddled with a gold link to the watch peeking from his vest pocket before continuing. "Three children survived Colonel Havens. Cole Havens, the oldest son, is now Master of Havenswood. Unfortunately, he does not have his father's instincts for farming. Jane is about your age, I would guess. And the

4

youngest boy, Henry, is all of twelve and a spit fire. He certainly needs a steadying hand as well as proper tutoring. A governess of your stature would put Havenswood back on an even track again."

Porter leaned forward, hands on the desk. "You will meet them all, of course, and then decide for yourself as to whether you choose to accept the position or not. I will be delighted to drive you out to the estate myself."

"Oh, that would be very kind of you, Mr. Porter."

He nodded, secure that he had closed the matter. "Now, if I may peruse your references and proper recommendations, please. I cannot recommend a finer opportunity for a lady of your obvious qualifications."

Miss Stiles cast him a warm gaze.

"Well, sir, you hardly know me, but I do thank you for your kindness." She opened a very worn carpetbag and removed two envelopes and handed them across to Porter.

He took them and proceeded to pull a pince-nez from his vest pocket and perched it atop his long nose, reading quickly but with care. In one envelope, bearing the address of the Perkins Law Offices in New York, was a letter of recommendation praising the efficiency of Miss Stiles as a clerk and personal secretary as well. The remaining letter in the first envelope was no less stellar. The typing school, Miss Robert's School for Typing Skills, recommended Emma Stiles to any and all potential employers. Miss Stiles received the highest grade in her certificate upon graduation.

The second envelope was a personal document. A letter from one Pastor Benjamin Adcock, of the First Baptist Congregation of Fifth Parish, New York City, affirmed the pure habits and grace of Emma Stiles.

Peter Porter could not contain the smile of satisfaction that crossed his face. He returned the envelopes to her, totally convinced that Miss Stiles was perfect for the Havens.

"Your references are impeccable and indisputable, Miss Stiles. I dare say you must be proud of them. I must ask, have you performed any governess duties in your accomplished work history?"

She gazed at him directly, a rueful smile. It added a touch of wistful beauty to her face.

"Well, I mentioned earlier that I was orphaned before the age of fourteen. I was placed with the Austin House for Homeless Children. Since I was much older than many of the other children there, the head mistress encouraged me into supervising much of the activities for the children. I was given the responsibility over many of the younger ones. I gained their trust easily and was quite good at it. It was rewarding, Mr. Porter, I must say. I believe I get along very well with younger children."

Porter nodded. "Well, young Henry is a handful, I won't deny that. He runs wild over the family. Cole and Jane have always done their best. Sad tale about Mrs. Havens. She died of consumption long ago. Old Colonel Havens did his best to bring up his children on his own, but it just isn't the same without a woman, I suppose. There are two family retainers living at Havenswood, Gabe and Hannah Browne. They are down to earth and kind. Hannah has attempted to take the place of Mrs. Havens with the rearing of the kids, but she is getting on in years and tired. Time is ripe for the right woman to step up and manage the young Henry. A woman like yourself..."

He paused, looking at her closely. "I know that both Cole and Jane Havens are most welcoming. Jane would be especially interested in a female companion..." He paused again, awkwardly attempting to find the words. "There are things women like to converse about, if you know what I mean."

"Yes, I do," she said. "I very much look forward to meeting the Havens."

Porter slapped his hands on the desk.

"Good, then. The only thing left is for you to see Havenswood for yourself, meet the family, and make your decision. As a matter of fact, I should drive you out to Havenswood myself and have you meet Cole. He had fairly given up hope that I would be able to find him a suitable person for the position."

"Oh, dear," Emma Stiles murmured. "My luggage at the boarding house—"

"Time enough for that," Porter said.

"But you see, Mr. Porter, I already paid for the week's lodging. Do you suppose—"

He shook his head. "Might I suggest, Miss Stiles, that we go to see Cole. If you both reach an agreement, I shall gladly take care of getting your things picked up and your money refunded. If not, then you will still have your room and a place to stay. I can almost assure you Miss Stiles, that if you choose not to work for the Havens, that I can find other employment for you here in Havens Falls. A woman of your qualifications is rare in these parts and I'll be darned if I will allow you to slip through our fingers." He smiled widely.

Emma Stiles laughed, a sound lovely and fresh. "Mr. Porter, are you always so kind and generous to strangers?"

His eyes twinkled as he shook his head. "No, not so to everyone, Miss Stiles, but you are too agreeable to gaze upon and an old war veteran like me never questions the workings of Providence. When you arrived, it was for a reason, I am sure, and I intend to make it near impossible for you to leave."

7

"Well, sir, you already have," she smiled and gazed at him with level sincerity.

"Come, then," Porter said, rising quickly. "We mustn't let grass grow under our feet. My rig is at the stables just behind the building across the street. Havenswood is just over a half hour's ride from here." He pulled out the gold watch from his vest. "We should be at Havenswood about noon." He chuckled. "If we're lucky, they may even invite us to dine with them."

Miss Stiles remained quiet, smoothing out the faint crease in her skirt and pulling her hat further down, while Porter searched about his office for his cane. As much as he loved his library of old leather and beloved Blackwoods and the earthy smell of the knotty pine that lined his walls, he regretted how messy his office appeared. His cracked and beaten wastepaper basket was overflowing with paper and discarded foolscap. He was at least thankful he had run out of cigars before Miss Stiles had graced his place. The strong whiff of cigars might have overwhelmed her and run her out before even conducting business.

He found his cane behind a bookcase and moved forward, holding open the wooden gate which separated his desk and office from the foyer. Miss Stiles walked quietly before him, nodding as she did so. Peter Porter adjusted his blue cravat haphazardly, set his hat upon his head and followed her. He rushed ahead to open the glass front door for Miss Stiles and they both stepped into the bright Pennsylvania sunshine.

Havens Falls was quiet and lazy before high noon. Along the rutted main thoroughfare, a buckboard moved at a slow pace, its wheels barely audible as they rolled in the worn grooves of the road. There was a blacksmith across the road, and the sound of hammer on anvil rang

8

through the late morning atmosphere. Porter offered his arm as they walked.

"Havens Falls has grown quickly," he said. "This town started as a place to come and sell your produce and general goods. Wagons gathered and it became a depot of sorts, until the settlers came in droves, bringing their families to settle permanently. Homes sprung up and a community was born." He paused and waved a hand in the air. "Now, we have a doctor, an honest to goodness qualified surgeon from New York, several dentists and even a circus tent a short distance away." Peter Porter was very proud of his town.

Emma Stiles looked about her and smiled sweetly back at Porter. "It doesn't seem so very big, Mr. Porter."

He cast an amused look at her, not able to resist marveling at the beauty of her profile. She looked like a delicate cameo, stoic and dignified. He couldn't help but smile.

"Two thousand souls at last count, my dear lady. Since the railroad gifted us with a regular stop, Havens Falls has burst with activity. Seems like the South, the West and everyone else want our apples, corn and peaches. And just wait until we start mining the coal at top capacity. There's more found each day."

"I believe you could be right, Mr. Porter."

He nodded and smiled, warmed by the pleasure her compliment afforded him. He stole secret glances of her as they walked across the street, and could not suppress a low sigh. His dear, sweet Carolina had been gone so long that he'd reverted to acting like an old fool over a young beauty.

They'd rounded an alleyway and Porter pressed her elbow in the narrow alley.

"Ah, here is my beauty, Miss Stiles. My pride and joy."

It was a handsome rig: a four wheeler with leather interior and shiny, polished gilt trim that ran the length of the sides. Someone took great care of the rig which sported a canopied roof.

"If you wait a moment, Miss Stiles, I will see about the horses. I promise I won't be long. We should be at Havenswood soon."

Emma Stiles, her face glowing in the sunshine, smiled approvingly. "I look forward to the trip, Mr. Porter. It has been a long time since I looked forward to anything more."

Porter looked at her, not sure how to respond, and cleared his throat, saying nothing. He moved quickly toward the stable building next door, his dirtied boots leaving a trail of dust behind.

Once the horses had been harnessed, Porter helped Miss Stiles into the leather seat of the carriage. She placed a heel on the metal foot rest and settled gently into position. Porter sat beside her, riding whip in hand. With a twinkle in his eyes and hat firmly on his head, he smiled.

"Off we go, my dear."

Emma Stiles smiled in return. "This is extraordinarily kind of you, Mr. Porter," she said softly.

"Bah. It is all my pleasure." He flicked the whip and the horses lurched forward.

"On to Havenswood, then," Emma said. "It has a lovely sound to it."

Porter nodded in agreement. "I do hope you can accept the position of governess there. It will give this old man great pleasure to please both the Havens family and such a lovely young woman as yourself."

She lowered her head shyly. "With all my heart, I hope they will accept me, Mr. Porter."

Delighted with the Pennsylvania countryside, the horses continued to move the carriage forward at a brisk pace

Chapter 2

Jane Havens had seen happier times. Not even the wisteria blooming behind Havenswood gladdened her aching heart. The abundant colors of purple, blue and white of the climbing flower could not change her melancholy mood. She only remembered how deeply her father, Colonel Havens, had loved the colorful climbing vines. He never saw weakness in a fierce man enjoying such gentle and frail things. It was she now, who tended the plants. Her father was long gone. She too, loved them the same, passionate way. Gabe and Hannah appreciated them too. But then, they had been with Havenswood in its glory days, when her father and mother first built it, when the land yielded its rich harvest of grain and other crops. Although the wisteria remain unchanged and bloomed each year, all else had changed. Withered.

She'd reached the seasoned age of twenty-three. Jane had been nearly a child when her mother died. Then her father, after having survived and born the battle scars of the Civil War, was stricken with a heart attack while riding his favorite horse, "Spirit," out behind Havenswood. He'd grown fond of taking long rides across the rolling hills that flanked Havenswood. One day, he never came back. Gabe went out and found him on the ground, Spirit looking over him.

Since then, Jane watched, with the eyes of a child and then of a grown woman, the decay of Havenswood. It was apparent to her that without a firm-handed master or mistress, the house had also died. Both she and Cole had failed.

Not that she was an ungrateful young woman. She thanked the Good Lord for her older brother, Cole, and her younger sibling, Henry. They had become her anchors, as were dear Gabe and Hannah. But the house—Havenswood—something went horribly wrong with the house. It seemed to have lost the will to exist after the death of her father. The few layers of watered down paint that the hired workers applied every other year never seemed to stick. The house retained the same, weathered, haunted and decayed look.

Jane sighed as she picked at the blue wisteria she'd gathered. It was no different this year. She and Cole worried how they would deal with their problems. The crops had failed again after the strong frost they'd experienced in the winter. It had gripped the entire valley. Certainly, she couldn't blame Cole or herself for that. But it had only added to his other excuses for drinking too much. Lately, he spent more time under the influence than not. Jane could not fathom why an intelligent, eligible and talented man like her brother could waste his vitality and his mind on the comforts from a bottle?

Cole was an artist and a poet. He had genuine talent. She believed he could sell his paintings and find publishers for his works of poetry. That income would help with the burden of the house maintenance. But now, because of the liquor, his hand was too unsteady to paint and his brain too foggy to pen poetry. And his temper worsened with the alcohol. He ranted and raved at the few workers they could afford, and even poor Gabe did not escape his wrath. Jane stood up to his bullying manner when she could. Gabe Browne was nearly seventy and not as spry as he once was.

Yes, Havenswood had once been a beautiful home, the envy of the land. It stood high atop a foothill, the border of West Virginia stretching out at a distance to the south. The white painted structure contrasted with its red dormer windows and gables reaching for the sky. Trellised porches, adorned with climbing vines and tall pilasters made for a breathtaking picture. A strong, old house built to withstand time. And yet...

No, Havenswood was no longer the fine, shining beauty on the hill, the gem that her victorious father, Colonel Vincent Havens, had built. The balls and parties and carriages filled with the famous and wealthy Pennsylvania families that came calling were gone. Jane feared they were gone for good.

She did not wish to let the self-pity wash over her once again. She peered down at her hands and nearly cried. Her hands, once soft and smooth, were now roughened from the field work she had done. With no extra money for frivolous extravagances, she'd learned to do without some of the feminine things and niceties to which most young ladies of her stature were accustomed to. No fancy, sweet smelling soaps or scented water or creams. No new bows or lace or satin ribbons.

Also, her youngest brother, Henry, was a hellion. He took every ounce of energy she had. He was most sorely in need of a strong and fierce hand to keep him in check. In a way, she resented Cole for not taking this task upon himself. He was the eldest male, heir and master of Havenswood now. It was his duty, she thought, to set an example for Henry. Cole should have stepped up and taken Henry under his tutelage. But no, he had turned to the bottle of spirits instead. He preferred to wallow in failure.

Jane's dresses of velvet and satin had faded to embarrassment, to where she often refused invitations to parties and dances. No amount of needlework could save or restore them to their former glory. Being the only daughter, she'd been saddled with the household duties, with little help, since Hannah was getting on in age. Jane Havens was not a happy young woman. She found very little desire to be within the walls of Havenswood.

She grudgingly began a slow walk back from the gardens to the house. The garden was her only respite from the dreariness of her life. It was enclosed by a grouping of matching-sized boulders, painted a brilliant white to make the path easy to follow by moonlight. There was a brick-walled well in the center. The garden was the heart of Havenswood and something Gabe, with Jane's help, was able to keep vibrant and alive.

The hot sun had tired her more than she realized and she hastened her step to the indoor shade. It was nearing noon and there was dinner to see to for Cole and Henry. It was Hannah Browne who cooked the meals but it was up to Jane, as young mistress of Havenswood, to oversee preparations.

Jane nearly walked into Hannah, who'd been in a rush to meet her.

"Oh, miss, there you are." The housekeeper wore a coarse woolen skirt, a white shirt waist, and plaid shawl over her shoulders. "We are entertaining visitors. Your brother wants to see you." Her expression was excited with the news.

"Cole wants to see me?"

"Yes, miss," Hannah said, flapping her shawl around to fan herself. "It's the lawyer, Mr. Porter. But he's got a young lady with him."

Jane's eyes lit up. She lost some of the melancholy that had gripped her earlier.

15

"Mr. Porter has come to visit? How nice. I so enjoy seeing the dear man. Where are they now?"

"In the main sitting room, Miss Jane. Hurry along. You know how impatient Master Cole is."

Jane, excitement growing, lifted her skirts slightly, to not impede her steps. She and Hannah had shared secrets and desires, life and disappointments since Jane was a young teen. Hannah had brought her the wisdom of learning how to accept life and get over things that could never be. Jane paused briefly.

"Who is the young lady?" she asked.

"Said her name was Emma Stiles."

"Is she pretty, Hannah? My age?" Jane's heart burned with interest. She would so welcome another young lady to converse with about feminine matters. Cole and Henry were not women.

Hannah folded her hands in front of her and nodded her head. "She is young, miss, but not as young as you. Is she pretty? Well, that is not how I would describe her, miss. I've never seen a woman as beautiful as Emma Stiles, miss." She hesitated. "But in an odd way."

"But how do you mean, Hannah?"

"She is dark, child. And I don't mean being colored. She is pale. Lean. But she has that darkness about her, like the gypsies that came through here last year. Why not see what you think of her. Go on and get along to the main room. Quick, now." She urged Jane on with her hands.

Jane only smiled. "I think you're a witch yourself, Hannah Browne." She finished with a giggle.

Hannah pointed a crooked finger at her. "Don't be going around saying such things, missy. Maybe I am, but I know what I see with my heart."

Jane dismissed her with a playful laugh and watched the older housekeeper bustle off toward the kitchen pantry hallway, her rough woolen skirts rustling. Jane hurried toward the sitting room, her thoughts all jumbled. Peter Porter was here for an unexpected visit and he had a guest with him. What could it possibly signify? She knew Mr. Porter was one of the greatest friends to the Havens family. Cole had briefly mentioned the idea of a substantial loan to tide them over the present crop failure and difficulties. That could explain Mr. Porter. But who was Emma Stiles? Well, there was no sense in speculating. She would have her answers when she met her.

They awaited her in the main sitting room—Cole, Mr. Porter and a tall, very slender woman in the most scrumptious hat Jane had seen in a long time. Emma Stiles. Jane rushed into the room, breathless, hardly able to conceal her elation. Would Mr. Porter and Emma Stiles be staying for lunch? She desperately wanted them to. Cole must invite them. There was food enough for all, even if she and Cole took smaller portions. It had been so long since they'd set a nice table for company.

"Where have you been, Jane?" Cole demanded, standing beside the winged chair that was his favorite in the room. "Perchance daydreaming again in the garden?"

Jane had long ago grown accustomed to his ill temper and impatience, but she still resented it slightly, especially today in the presence of their guests. Yet she could not be angry at her brother for long.

"I apologize, Cole." Her gaze met her brother's and then darted to the tall woman in the hat. "I was tending to the wisterias. Do forgive me—" She glanced at the lovely stranger again. "—Everyone."

She moved to Mr. Porter. "It is so good to see you, Mr. Porter. So good of you to visit." Jane put out a hand in greeting.

Peter Porter bowed and took her hand. "How are you, my dear Jane? You are lovely as always."

17

"Yes, as lovely and as unpunctual as always, too," Cole said, a slight grin playing on his face.

To a stranger's eyes, Cole Havens was romantically stylish and handsome. His dark, tousled hair swept carelessly across his forehead, contrasted his tanned skin. He spent much time in the fields. Not even the dreadful bouts with the demon alcohol could take away his debonair look.

But it wasn't her brother who stole her attention. She had not been properly prepared for the sight of Emma Stiles. Jane was totally lost to Peter Porter's introduction until she heard Miss Stiles' deep, fluid voice.

"I am so happy to meet you, Miss Havens."

Jane was literally blinded by the dazzling Miss Stiles.

"Oh, I am equally delighted," Jane stammered. "I do hope Cole thought to offer both of you refreshments, tea, cakes—"

"He has indeed offered," Peter Porter chuckled. "However, we refused." His smile broadened. "You see, we are staying for dinner instead. You are stuck, I'm afraid, with full luncheon duties."

Jane blushed, excitement flushing her cheeks red. They were staying! Even Cole seemed happy to have guests. She also noticed how his eyes never left the person of Miss Stiles.

"Excellent idea, Cole. Miss Stiles, I'm so looking forward to our dinner conversation," Jane said, trying to contain her enthusiasm as best she could. A lady could not bubble over in public. She cast her gaze upon their female guest. "I do hope you like roast chicken, Miss Stiles."

"I do. It is one of my favorites." Emma smiled at her.

Jane had not realized she'd been staring at the beautiful woman until Cole cleared his throat.

"Jane?"

She redirected her gaze to her older brother, yet her mind dwelled on Hannah's observations about Miss Stiles. What darkness had Hannah seen in this radiant face? Dark indeed! Hannah's opinion bordered on ridiculous. Miss Stiles was as fair, and stunning as the picture of the Madonna in the Holy Bible. Of course, the fullness of Miss Stile's lips added a touch of worldliness about her, but that only added to her sheer elegance and beauty. Gypsy indeed. Jane had never seen another woman as magnificent as Emma Stiles. On that matter, Hannah had it right. And Jane was on pins and needles wondering the reason for her presence in Havenswood.

"Jane," Cole said again, breaking the spell, "What say you to a governess for Henry?" He was smiling.

"Well," Jane said, trying to control the beating in her chest. "I'm sure you know what is best for Henry."

"Of course. Through Mr. Porter's good search, we were fortunate to have found a more than suitable governess for our little brother. Perhaps Miss Stiles can help us tame his wild streak." He looked at Emma Stiles again. "I think that she can."

Jane could scarcely control her emotions. Another woman in Havenswood! A young and beautiful woman. A woman to talk to, confide in and take up the hours in this dull old house. It would go a long way to making life worth waking up to.

"Oh, Cole, I just don't know what to say."

Peter Porter smiled wide. "Well, my dear, just say you approve of the idea and it's done. It would please me to know I've done the right thing for you and your brother by bringing Miss Stiles here."

Emma Stiles put her hand gently on Jane's shoulder. "I would not think of accepting the position if you did not want me." Her smile penetrated into Jane's still thudding heart.

"Oh, but yes...of course," Jane said, and clasped Miss Stiles gloved hand in hers. "It's a wonderful idea. I thought we would never find someone to come and help us with Henry."

"Good, then it's settled," Cole muttered, sounding final. "Now, Jane, why not run off to the kitchen and see if Hannah needs help and check on the roast chicken as well while I pour Mr. Porter a glass of his favorite sherry. It would not be a proper visit, am I correct, Mr. Porter, without the indulgence?" He turned to Miss Stiles. "You see, it was my father's custom to share an aperitif with his old friend before a meal. He taught me that it stimulates the appetite and aids in digestion." Cole poured sherry for Mr. Porter, and then for himself. "And now it is my custom as well, because my father was a brilliant man." He raised his glass in a friendly toast. "To you, good sir"

Jane took off in a near run, hardly caring to hear her brother's incessant tales. She gathered the hem of her skirt and headed toward the kitchen, her heart thundering in her ears. She had to see about the roast chicken, of course, but her mind, her thoughts, were of Emma Stiles.

A governess for Henry.

A friend for herself!

She silently thanked God. Things were improving around Havenswood. Miss Emma Stiles made it so.

Chapter 3

*T*he afternoon meal was served in the main dining room. It was a dinner Jane would never forget. The room, the table setting, the entire occasion had taken on an air of such pleasure. It had been too long since she could recall a happier affair. Jane could not remember the last time Havenswood had entertained guests. To her delight, Cole was exceptionally charming and gracious. He was in total command as head of the house. If only she could keep him this happy and away from the drink.

Jane had always loved the main dining room, but today, it positively glowed. The deep walnut walls glistened with wax, and the matching portraits of their parents, Colonel Havens and Sarah Havens, appeared alive in the candlelight. It was as if they looked down to cast their approval upon their children. The Colonel's Union Blue uniform was adorned with epaulettes and gold buttons, and his dark hair and sweeping moustache were bold. His painting dominated the room. Sarah Havens' more subdued painting spoke with a more quiet charm. Her dainty, cameo face and tender, pale skin contrasted with the deep red of her gown.

Jane couldn't help but admire the large, hanging chandelier with its dangling crystals that glittered and

21

bedazzled the room. Had Hannah or Gabe cleaned it recently, or did everything just look more beautiful because of her good feeling? The velvet drapes on the windows were pulled back, offering a clear view of the hills off in the distance.

Miss Stiles sat still and perfectly poised in the ornate chair. Jane noticed how Cole eyed her with satisfaction. How could he not find the new governess totally captivating? Had she not herself been smitten entirely? Peter Porter was busily enjoying the vegetable soup.

"I'm certain you will be happy with your stay here," Jane said. "It might take you a while to get used to Henry's ways. He can be more than a handful at times."

Cole snorted. "But he is only a boy with excess spirit. Better an abundance of that than a mewling child cowering at his shadow and running to have his tears wiped away at any little stumble."

Mr. Porter chuckled. "Much like another wild boy I remember well." He winked at Cole. "He's managed to grow out of his troubled childhood."

"Well, my father managed me with care," Cole replied.

"I don't suppose to dispute that, my boy," Mr. Porter said softly.

"And where might my young ward be at the moment? Emma asked.

Jane dabbed the corner of her mouth with a delicate dinner napkin. "I suppose he is out hunting for frogs or some other vulnerable beast with the Simpson boys. They are the same age as Henry and their estate is about a quarter of a mile further down the road to the west."

"Ah, frogs," said Miss Stiles. "Boys learn a great deal from them at his age." She had a slight smile as she looked at Jane.

Cole Havens changed the subject. "So, Miss Stiles, you say you speak two languages. That is something to be envied. Which languages, if I may inquire?"

"Spanish and French, Mr. Havens."

Cole reached for the glass of sherry, holding it to his lips. "I see you favor the romantic languages." He took a sip. "There should be more romance in the world, don't you think, Miss Stiles? That is why poets expend so much ink and paper on it and painters so much paint on canvas depicting love's pain and pleasure." His gaze settled on her.

"Perhaps, Mr. Havens, poets and painters are best equipped to put romance into perspective." She avoided his gaze and look directly into Jane's eyes. "Perhaps our passions for romance should be more privately shared and admired."

"Indeed," Cole said almost bitterly, refilling his glass with more sherry and downing it in one swallow.

Peter Porter sliced methodically through the roast chicken on his plate. "Cole, are you painting again? Or still thinking about it?"

Cole smirked at Porter across the table.

"I pick up a brush now and again. I have no hopes that it will amount to much. I merely dabble, that is all. Hard to take something as serious as painting when all my time is taken up with this house." He looked around the room.

Jane noted the pain so evident in her brother's voice. Porter nodded as he chewed. "True enough, my man. However, you're still a young man. With your talent, you should pursue it. Find the time." He turned to Jane. "Am I right, Jane?"

She nodded enthusiastically. "Oh, yes, I agree. Cole's paintings are ever so grand. I'm no expert, of course, but he really is talented. His portrait of Henry is alive with color and life." She turned to Cole. "Cole, you must show Mr. Porter your painting."

Cole only growled. "Let's end this matter now. I do not want to bore Miss Stiles with talk of something as insignificant as my paintings."

The remark was rude and Peter Porter leveled a look of disappointment at him. Jane looked down at her plate, not knowing what to say. But Miss Stiles looked steadily at Cole, seeming unfazed by his improper comment.

"Would it be possible to see your paintings sometime?

Cole only shrugged. "If you really want to, sure." He downed another glass of sherry.

The conversation over Cole's artwork seemed to have relaxed everyone, despite his attempt to bring it to nearly an abrupt end. The sherry appeared to have taken the edge off him, but he had imbibed too much already. Jane and Mr. Porter encouraged Emma Stiles to talk about herself. It was then that Jane learned of her life as an orphan and eventual employment in New York. Jane sat spellbound, marveling at all the things this strong woman had accomplished. For all of Emma's tender years, she had mastered the world in Jane's eyes.

The pleasant conversation might have continued long after Hannah had cleared the table had not Cole suddenly pushed back from his chair and rose unsteadily to his feet. He'd obviously had too much sherry. This was painfully obvious to Jane, and she was certain both Mr. Porter and Emma Stiles were equally aware. He usually managed to retain enough control to conduct himself like a gentleman, but Jane waited for him to erupt and ruin the entire special occasion.

"Cole, no—" she said as she put out a hand to him. She stopped when she suddenly realized he wasn't listening to her. He stood silent, staring right past her, his eyes aflame

24

with anger. He was looking toward the arched entrance to the dining room. Jane and the others followed his gaze.

Suddenly, Cole's jarringly loud laughter filled the room.

"Well, now," he said, "Our young Henry and his ever faithful mutt are done with their scampering about the countryside." His eyes clouded over and his face contorted. "You are a young scamp! How dare you take off without permission and not show up for dinner?" Cole pointed to the muddied and dirty golden retriever, Goldy, hugging the boy's legs. "And you will be responsible for bathing that dog before you get any supper tonight."

Jane, breaking the shock she'd found herself in, rose from the chair and swiftly ran to her little brother's side, patting Goldy's head. Poor Henry, he looked so frail and thin standing there in fear of Cole's fury. For all his unruly, wild hair and freckles, he was the spitting image of their father, except he had been blessed with his mother's fair hair.

Apparently, little Henry had gone off wearing only a green shirt and blue overalls. It had not been enough to guard against the brambles and thickets of the woods. His shirt and overalls were torn in several places. He shrunk against Jane's skirt.

"I'm very sorry, Cole," he said in a thin, high voice. "Me and Big Willie found this gopher hole—"

"Henry Havens," Jane said as sternly as she could pretend. "Coming home after dinner is served is not encouraged and especially not when we have company, but coming in here looking like the Wrath of God—" She halted, not wanting to scold him too severely. She smiled and winked at him instead. "Well, come on in then, since you have arrived, and say hello to Mr. Porter and..." She paused, briefly eyeing the gaunt and lovely Emma Stiles. "There is someone you will want to meet."

25

He looked up at her with sparkling blue eyes. "But golly, Janey, you should'a seen the size of the gopher."

"Never you mind the gophers. And your English is atrocious, young man." She led him to the table, though he attempted desperately to hold back. Goldy followed obediently behind them.

Cole glared at him, but Jane knew that he was not too genuinely angry at Henry. The twinkle in his eyes betrayed him.

"Very well," Cole finally said. "You may be as dirty as that straggly dog of yours, but you are kin after all. And we have done something especially for you." He pointed to Miss Stiles. "This is Miss Emma Stiles. She is to be your governess and will be staying with us here at Havenswood."

"Governess?" he echoed. "You don't mean—a teacher?" He suddenly shrank even further behind Jane.

Miss Stiles smiled directly at Henry.

"Hello, Henry. I am very delighted to meet you."

He lowered his eyes and only nodded. Peter Porter let out a laugh.

"Well, young man, if I were your age, I would be only too eager to learn with the likes of Miss Stiles."

"Yes, sir," Henry mumbled, looking not at Porter but at Miss Stiles.

"Well, speak up Henry," Cole commanded, the slur evident in his words. "I'll wager Miss Stiles will make a proper gentleman out of you. The Lord knows I've tried and failed."

Miss Stiles ignored Cole's outburst, folded her hands together and set her attention on Henry.

"Tell me, Henry, did you catch many frogs today?"

Suddenly, the boy's head came up and a slight smile formed on his dirtied face. "Who told you about that?" he asked carefully.

"Well, your sister Jane mentioned something. Was it a secret?"

He shook his head slightly. "Not really..."

"Oh, I like frogs too," she said. "I used to have a big, spotted one back home. It was not the prettiest frog. All green and brown like a bad salad. You know the kind?" She had a very serious look.

He eyed her without suspicion and frowned.

"Yeah, I've seen those kind. Plenty of them down at the pond. But we didn't go there today. Big Willie saw the giant gopher hole and we decided to try and catch one to see if we could see his shadow. You know about that?" His question was almost a whisper.

"Indeed, I do. But I'm afraid you and your friend are a bit too late in the year for the gopher's shadow. You can only see it in early spring, but best at late winter, on a bright, sunny day."

Henry's eyes grew wide. "Gosh, you know everything."

Emma gave her little brother one of the most fetching smiles Jane Havens had ever seen.

"I know a little," Miss Stiles said. "You see, Henry, when I was younger and lived..." She paused, and Jane saw a darkness cloud her eyes, but it passed quickly. "I lived deep in the woods in a small house. We had all kinds of wild animals as neighbors."

"Wow," Henry exclaimed. "You did?" The amazement in his voice was genuine. Jane was overjoyed. How could anyone who met Emma Stiles not succumb to her charms? She could see the rapport that was already deepening between her little brother and Miss Stiles. If she could develop a trusting relationship with Henry, their problems with him could turn out to be a thing of the past.

Even Cole caught the change in Henry. He cast an approving glance at Jane and Peter Porter.

"Time to say your farewells for now, Henry," Cole said. "See that you get Gabe to help you wash up Goldy and then you do the same and make yourself tidy. I'll see Mrs. Browne about setting up a place for you at the table. Are you hungry?"

"Oh, yes, Cole."

"Fine, then. Jane, would you take Miss Stiles back to the sitting room? We shall have coffee and brandy there." He turned to Mr. Porter. "I'm sure you will be returning to your office soon? I wouldn't wish to detain you."

"Indeed, my good man. Work still awaits me there." He looked at his pocket watch. " Good Lord, but it is nearly three already. It'll have to be a quick drink, Cole."

"Better quick than not at all."

As Jane guided Emma into the hallway, Henry scampered up the grand staircase, with Goldy at his heels. Jane caught him glancing back at his new governess one more time before he disappeared upstairs. She still marveled at how easily the new governess had bonded with Henry.

"Miss Stiles," she said, "That was a brilliant manner in handling my little brother. He took an immediate liking to you, and understood that you were interested in his world. That you want to be his friend and not just an authoritarian figure."

The governess nodded. "Miss Havens, it's true that he is still just a boy," she said, "but as with all children, he doesn't like being treated as one. It is not difficult to calculate." She flashed a most disarming smile at Jane.

Jane did not shy away from the eye contact. "I find myself quite willing to believe anything after seeing you with him. I've had no problem getting on with Henry, but when it comes to disciplining him, I'm afraid I've failed as surely as Cole has. Once he gives me his puppy-dog eyes, my resolve melts."

Miss Stiles laughed lightly and Jane's inside trembled with joy.

"Yes, I noticed that he is well aware of ways to charm you and take advantage of it. Children his age are very adept at manipulation. They could teach us a thing or two."

Jane sighed audibly, shaking her head slightly as they reached the doors of the sitting room.

"I am ashamed to ask, but I am filled with curiosity. How came you to hold so much wisdom for someone so—" She hesitated, befuddled on how to be polite and still ask her question.

"One so what, Miss Havens?" She pressed Jane's arm gently.

Jane's heart fluttered like a bird ready to take flight. Would she be able to utter coherent thoughts? Why was this woman having such an effect on her?

"Well...It is just that you are so young. I don't imagine you are too much older than me, yet it surprises and amazes me that you have already accomplished so much and acquired such vast wisdom."

Emma Stiles paused before the closed doors. For a fleeting moment, Jane thought she sensed a mood change in the young woman. Her eyes shadowed a touch of anger. Jane feared she had pressed her too far with her questions.

"Miss Havens, I have lived a more complicated life than most. Upbringing can create scars or it can create harmony. I've often felt more kinship with children because of my own losses. You see, I lost my parents when at a tender age. I did not understand my loss then. Perhaps that is why I reach out to children and they respond."

Impulsively, Jane reached out and took both of the other woman's hands.

"My dear, Miss Stiles, we are blessed that you have come to us and Henry will be very fortunate to have you." She could not stop herself. "And how wonderful for me, too." She blushed, suddenly ashamed of her boldness.

Emma Stiles acknowledged her confession with a slight smile and a gaze that was both intense yet distant.

She did not withdraw her hands from Jane's hold.

***

There was disorder in the Havenswood kitchen. Hannah Browne begrudged the arrival of Emma Stiles. She did not view the governess with great enthusiasm. Indeed, when her husband, Gabe, came in from the barn in search of saddle soap for the harness rigs and saddles, he was quick to note the sour and bitter mood of his wife. Since Hannah was generally a cheerful woman, she was positively grim today.

"Hannah, are you doing poorly?" Gabe asked her.

"It be nothing you could do."

"Well, let me be the judge of that. Out with it, now. You look as sweet as a sour persimmon. What happened? Everything straight with the family?"

Hannah plunged a china plate into the soapy water in the kitchen sink. Without looking at her husband, she remarked, "Have you seen that new governess for Henry?"

"You mean that lady that rode in with Mr. Porter?"

"Yes, that's her."

Gabe pulled on his short, gray beard. "Mighty pretty, that lady. Hard to miss." He smiled.

Hannah placed the plate on her right, where it would dry on the rack, pulled out another plate from the sink and began scrubbing.

"Sure, she is lovely. But I don't care for her."

"Have you talked to her already?"

"Course not. Don't need to."

"Did she put on airs around you?"

"No."

Her husband shook his head. "Then what in tarnation do you have against the lady?"

Hannah paused from her scrubbing. "She just doesn't sit well with me." She looked steadily at him. "You know me, Gabe. You know how I am. I get these feelings. I get bad feelings about her. I think she may well bring bad luck to this house and the Good Lord knows we don't need any more bad luck round this place."

Her husband faltered under her hard stare. "Why do you say things like that, Hannah?"

"She's a dark one, I tell you," his wife whispered strongly. "There is something fey about her. Something not right." She pointed a finger at Gabe. "You know I had the same feelings about the gypsies that came through town last year. And sure enough, they robbed poor Mrs. Munson, even after she kindly allowed them to camp on her land."

Women thought Gabe Browne. They never failed to confound him. Yet, he was aware that his wife did have uncanny instincts at times. But the way she was carrying on about Miss Stiles made him uncomfortable.

"Hannah, darling, why not wait and see how this Miss Stiles works out? You and I both know that boy could stand some discipline and schooling." He cleared his throat. "Now, how's about some coffee if there's any left on the boil? I'll be out with the harnesses till suppertime for certain."

She patted his arm lovingly. "Plenty of coffee left, Gabe."

The day was a warm one, yet Gabe Browne couldn't suppress the slight shiver in his old bones as he sipped his black coffee. He hoped Hannah was wrong this time.

31

Chapter 4

*J*ane's days had been magical since Emma's arrival at Havenswood. The entire house had undergone a transformation. Well, at least in Jane's eyes. She was especially elated when she found out that Cole had placed Emma Stiles in the empty room right across the hall from Henry's bedroom. Her own bedchamber was next to Henry's and Cole's large master bedroom, his sanctum sanctorum, on the other side of Henry's. That meant everyone would be settled within easy access to one another on the second floor of Havenswood.

Gabe and Hannah had rather large living quarters in the added wing just beyond the kitchen. They liked that they had their privacy. They were only a bell-pull away. Jane was relieved that the new governess hadn't been hidden away in some remote wing of the house. There was something alluring about the nearness of her. In her heart, Jane knew she was growing fonder of Emma Stiles.

The next day, Miss Stiles's luggage arrived from Wilkins House, along with a brown envelope containing every penny she had paid in advance. True to his word, Peter Porter had indeed taken care of everything for Miss Stiles.

Jane passed part of the afternoon watching the porters carry the new governess's portmanteau and other pieces up the main staircase. She was particularly taken with the large steamer trunk, studded with brass nails and gilded copper braces. She fantasized that it could be a pirate's spoils inside and that Emma Stiles was really a pirate in hiding. The only other pieces of luggage were a large suitcase and a rather worn carpet bag. That was the sum of Emma Stiles's worldly possessions.

What would it be like to be with her when she opened and unpacked that trunk? Jane let her imagination wander. Wistfully, she realized how much she missed the companionship of another woman closer to her age in her life. There was so much she wanted to discuss with Miss Stiles. She had lived and worked in New York. Everything was fashionable in New York, wasn't it? Fashion, society gossip, the arts—it all happened in New York. She hungered for any news Miss Stiles might share with her, and she sincerely hoped they would grow close and become good friends. That might be frowned upon by the old, stodgy elite, but Jane never prescribed to class distinction in her own home. She couldn't help but recall how quickly the woman had won over Henry. That made her extraordinarily special in Jane's eyes.

Once all the luggage was delivered and the men left, Jane knew her curiosity would get the best of her. She found herself standing in front of Miss Stiles's door. Would it be objectionable, she wondered, to ask if she might need help putting things away? Jane was surprised when the door opened before she could knock. Emma Stiles stood before her in a lovely lacy silk dress. The darkness of her hair and eyebrows set off the cream color of the dress. She eyed Jane with an amused smile.

"Won't you come in, Miss Havens. I've been unpacking, as you can see."

The brass-bound trunk sat on the floor, still untouched. The governess seemed to be concentrating on the contents of the carpet bag. Letters and assorted toiletry items lay scattered on the canopied, four-poster bed.

"I hope I am not intruding. I came to see if I might be of some help in putting things away, Miss Stiles."

The new governess closed the door and faced Jane, her piercing blue eyes fixed steadily on her.

"Thank you, Miss Havens, but I think I can manage. By the way, is it permissible in your household for you to call me Emma? We are going to become like family, in a way, while I live here, and I would love it if we could become friends."

Jane's heart leapt. "Oh, I so want us to become friends too." *Yes, I would love for my name to be on your lips.* Jane wanted nothing more. "Please, call me Jane."

Emma continued to watch her. "It shall be our secret."

Jane shrank from the intense gaze. A warm feeling coursed through her.

"By the way, I wanted to inform you that Cole has suggested that you use the library as a schoolroom for Henry. I am ashamed to admit we never set up a room just for his lessons. You are free to set your own schedule as well. We shall make sure he adheres to it." She smiled shyly.

Again, Emma said nothing, only stared.

"You will like the library," Jane continued, feeling at a loss for words. "The Colonel adored reading, despite his adventurous life. He especially enjoyed Shakespeare."

"The Colonel?" Emma murmured.

"My father," Jane said. "We all called him "the Colonel" affectionately. He was proud of the title. I almost never remember father without his uniform. You did see his portrait in the dining room?"

Emma nodded. "Ah, yes, I saw the portrait. He had fine character in his face. And please thank your brother, should you see him before I do. The library sounds ideal. A perfect place for learning."

"I just know that if anyone can teach our Henry anything, it is you, Miss Sti—Emma!" Jane effused enthusiasm.

"I thank you, Jane. I will strive to fulfill your confidence."

Jane moved closer to her.

"Emma," she said quietly, "I am not much good at etiquette or propriety and some say I can be too forward for a young lady, but you and I being nearly the same age and all, I think it would fine for us to dispense with titles indeed."

Emma moved even closer and Jane inhaled the sweet scent of lilac water. The governess extended her hands to Jane, never removing her eyes from Jane's face.

"How good that would be. I would very much like it if we could move beyond our stations. In the two days I've been here, I feel as if I've known you for longer and I hope we shall form a close friendship, Jane."

Jane felt her face go flush and she hoped the other woman would not see how red her cheeks were surely glowing. The sound of her name coming from Emma's lips was like sweet honey. It was far better than when Hannah called her by her given name.

"Oh, please don't let Cole know right away, though," Jane laughed. "He's still fond of informing me that I am not at all the proper lady I should be. And I don't mind him knowing of our friendship, only that he has been so stressed of late with so much to bear and then there is—"

She stopped short of blurting out Cole's drinking problem. It would cause him great shame if she'd revealed it to Emma. But the other woman looked at her with gentle eyes.

"Jane," she said quietly, "you are a very attractive young woman, sure to catch the eye of many a young man. If your brother does not take notice of your fine qualifications, I am certain it is only because he looks upon you only as his younger sister. Any other suitor will look upon you far differently."

Jane, thoroughly enthused at Emma's words, sat down on the fluffy edge of the bed.

"You are too generous with your words." Inside, she was thrilled. Emma Stiles thought her attractive.

Emma began to fold some of her items in the big drawers of the dresser.

"Has not some young man entertained a desire to marry you or even court you?"

Jane blushed again. She could not control it.

"None. And I don't really care to bring about such interest at the moment." She rose from the bed. "But I am going on like an unhappy parrot and you've so much unpacking to do. Please forgive me for taking up so much of your time. I should leave you now."

Emma stopped what she was doing and smiled. "Very well, Jane. We shall have an entire week to get acquainted before I begin a set schedule for Henry's studies. We must plan to spend some time together."

***

And that was how the magic began. Jane felt there was much that made Emma Stiles special. She could not pin point what it was and didn't much care. There were no rules of social behavior penned thus far that could apply to this woman. Emma. She repeated the name often while she was alone. What a lovely name.

And the magic was not just something only she felt. The first several days, Emma began simple test lessons with Henry. She started with the three Rs. Jane couldn't suppress the joy she felt. It was evident in every part of her being. Even Havenswood seemed to take on a new life despite the barren fields and the paint still peeling.

Jane would not listen to the doom and gloom voice of Hannah Browne, who remained aloof and not too kind toward Emma's influence at Havenswood. Jane hated to think it was jealousy but what else could it be? Hannah had looked after Henry and been like a mother to her. And now a new, very young, beautiful woman had come into the Havens' clan sporting elegance, wit and talent. It was perfectly natural that Hannah should turn sour on the new governess. Jane felt sure it would pass. She knew Hannah was a kind and gentle woman, and one with wisdom to spare.

One day that same week, as Jane passed the library on the way to the kitchen to check on the noon dinner, she suddenly stopped, caught by the light sound of Henry's laughter inside. Jane was properly brought up to never eavesdrop but she could not resist the temptation to find out what had made her little brother laugh so gleefully. The door was slightly ajar and she pressed her ear to it.

"—like a real owl. You do that so good. Do it again, please, Miss Stiles."

"Do that so _well_, Henry. That is the proper phrase. All right, but only just one more time."

From inside the library came the hoot of an owl. It sounded so real, Jane swore a wild owl had flown into the Havenswood library! She held her breath and smiled. How talented Emma was.

Henry attempted to make the same sound but was not as accomplished. Jane heard him clapping his hands.

"Yes, Henry, that is very good," Emma affirmed. "You have a very good ear, young man. I can see you have a love for the woods and the voices of nature. Heavens, I believe we've had enough bird calls for the day."

"Aw, no, Miss Stiles, couldn't we do more?"

"Your sad-eye looks will not work with me, Henry Havens. We must get down to more serious studies. We will study sentence structure next."

Not wanting to linger and get caught, Jane continued on to the kitchen, her spirits lifted and a song in her heart.

***

At first, Cole hadn't seemed to notice or care that the atmosphere had lifted within the walls of Havenswood. He continued to spend long hours closeted in the den with a bottle of brandy. Jane could hear him pacing in the room, sometimes slamming his fists together and muttering to himself. It was a Friday, and the large ornately carved Swiss clock in the hallway struck the four o'clock hour.

Alarmed, she entered the room and found her brother stretched out full-length in the old chair that faced the red brick fireplace. He was staring glumly at a pile of cold embers. The days had steadily become warmer. Sunshine-filled May days brought balmy breezes that promised a blossoming summer.

Cole's cravat lay crumpled and a mess on his chest, his uncombed hair rebellious around his face. His cheeks were flush and his chest heaved irregularly. When Jane approached him, he barely looked up or acknowledged her. She knew he would end up like this each time he found his way to this room. The den was a memento room to the Civil War and the Colonel's days as a Union officer. There were treasures belonging to their father like medals, captured bullet-ridden Confederate flags, and swords and guns.

38

"Have you come to give me grief, dear sister?" he demanded sullenly.

"Must you drink so early, Cole? It seems each day gets worse."

He turned awkwardly to look up at her.

"Yes, I must. It helps me forget how miserable my life really is."

Jane dropped suddenly to her knees, her auburn-tressed head on his lap. Cole didn't even touch her, but stared gloomily at the fireplace.

"Cole, you are wasting your life away on purpose. There is nothing in that—" She pointed to the nearly empty bottle on the table beside him. "There is nothing in that bottle but misery."

He shook his head. "You could never understand," he said curtly. "You're a woman."

Jane leaned back. "I am your sister and whether I understand or not, I love you," she declared proudly. "You are Master of Havenswood and should be ashamed of behaving like some drunkard in a town tavern. You owe it to the Havens name and legacy to keep your head about you. And we have a new person in the house too."

He uttered harsh laughter. "Imagine that, wisdom from the mouth of babes. My aim is not to make you ashamed of me, because I have no shame left for myself. But you see, dear Jane, I find it too hard to correlate who I am with who I was of late."

Jane gazed at him, concerned.

"Oh, Cole, please speak to me in plain words," she begged. "I so desperately need my brother back."

"Well, my dear sister, if it's brazen honesty you want, then I shall give you that. I am a total and abject failure. Is that clear enough for you, Jane? I am lost. Here I am, the son and heir of a great man, but look around..." He waved his arm wildly. "In the past ten years I have done nothing to build or add to the legacy he left us. Nothing." He looked at her with bloodshot eyes. "Father would probably throw me out of this God-damned house if he were alive today."

Jane could feel her anger and frustration building. "No! I won't have you say those things. You can be whatever you want to be."

He shoved her away and rose unsteadily to his feet, heading for the glass decanter on the side board. Jane knew it was useless to try and stop him. She had tried many times before. All she could do was watch as he poured himself another full glass.

He turned to her, held the glass up in salute and gulped it down.

"I don't need your sisterly concerns," he growled. "It's time we all faced the dirty little facts. Mr. Porter advanced us six hundred dollars to tide the estate over these months. And I wonder if you have any brilliant ideas about how to pay the good man back, dear sister, unless we have good crops this summer. You see, I am quite useless as a brother and a gentleman. I am a man with no useful skills. I can not create money. Old Gabe's a better man than I am."

"Stop it, Cole. You must stop speaking in this manner."

"Why don't you stop it," he said with a surprising softness in his slur. "Don't you understand, Jane, that we owe Peter Porter everything. He even found our Miss Stiles for us. I failed there too. I couldn't even be a positive voice in Henry's upbringing." He raised the near empty glass. "What else is there but this?"

"Your paintings. Your poetry."

His face twisted in anger again. "I plead with you, don't ever mention those things to me again. I forbid you to do so!"

40

Jane could see she had hit a raw nerve. Her brother was in a near rage now. His breathing was labored, and his chest heaved. She shuddered and stepped away from him. She wanted to cry but she had already shed all her tears for her brother. It sickened her heart, and she felt deep down inside that it would end badly. Seeing her brother like this was terrible, and she wished that Emma would never know how far gone to liquor her brother was.

He waved her away. "Leave me alone, Jane, please. I want to enjoy what I have left of this day in solitude."

Jane walked slowly to the door, once again defeated. Cole finished off the drink in his glass and headed back for more but a soft knock on the door stopped him.

"What now—?" he growled. "Come in, I can't stop you."

Emma Stiles entered, closing the door gently behind her. Jane was surprised at the sight of her and Cole stared, his jaw open in shock.

Emma held a canvas in her slender hands. It was a foot-square canvas that bore an oil likeness of Henry with his dog, Goldy. Jane recognized it as the painting Cole had done for Henry's room.

Cole did not remove his gaze from it, his hands curling into tight fists, too shocked and surprised to express the anger he obviously felt.

"And what is the purpose of that here?" He pointed to the portrait.

Emma's eyes sparkled. "Forgive me for the intrusion, but I just discovered this in Henry's room. He is very proud of it. I couldn't help but come to you straight away, Mr. Havens. I am so very impressed by your talent."

"Is that so, Miss Stiles?" Cole turned to the decanter. "And what does that mean?"

"I am saying, Mr. Havens, that you obviously are an artist of great promise. I fail to understand why you are not proud of your work. Your entire family should be quite proud of you."

He turned away, some of his drink spilling over onto the carpet.

"Miss Stiles," he warned, "I am not so drunk that I cannot recognize pure flattery."

She looked at him, perplexed by his reaction. Her gaze fell on Jane.

"I cannot imagine that a man who is capable of such work not see or appreciate his own artistry."

She held up the painting, facing Cole and Jane. They both stared at it, Jane marveling anew at Emma's power to charm and command. Henry's portrait was testimony enough. Through Cole's use of colorful brushstrokes and use of light, Henry and Goldy magically came alive on the canvas.

"Well, yes, it's good," Cole grudgingly admitted. "But you are being too fussy about it. Any dabbler could do as well."

"I think not," Emma Stiles said with a calm firmness. "Any dabbler could not paint such a living, breathing portrait. Only a true artist could have created this."

"Look, Miss Stiles, I do thank you for your extreme kindness, but I must ask that you please return the painting to my brother's room now."

Emma bowed her head and lowered the painting.

"Of course, Mr. Havens."

She finally turned away and walked out, closing the library door behind her. Cole stared sullenly after her.

Jane moved to the door, ready to follow Emma out.

"Jane," Cole called softly.

"Yes?"

"Did you believe her? I mean, do you really think I'm a real artist? Someone with real talent?"

Jane smiled. "Yes, Cole, I do. Have you never listened to me? I've told you so many times. Miss Stiles may be new and I have yet to make a friend of her, but I feel certain she is most certainly not a prevaricator."

"But what can she know of art? She is only a servant. A common governess."

No, not common. Special. Jane thought.

"Perhaps not so common, brother."

She turned quickly and left the library. Even as she heard the click of the door behind her, the sound of smashing glass against the fireplace sent a pang of pain through her heart.

Chapter 5

*J*ane had grown to love suppertime best in Havenswood. The disrepair and shabbiness of the house so clearly evident during the harsh daylight took on a magical aura all its own come nightfall. At dusk, the shadows grew long and heavy, filling every corner of the rambling Havenswood, leaving only the glowing heart of the house in view. Gabe Browne lit all the candlesticks, candelabras and chandeliers until Havenswood would glimmer and shimmer like an exotic jewel. The crystal chandelier gleamed. The oil studies along the wall came to life. The worn edges of the drapes and furniture even took on a look of newness and the mahogany shone with a rich darkness.

Jane could easily imagine the Colonel marching down the main stairs, while Mother followed, rocking little Henry in her weak arms. But only the ghosts were here now.

For some reason, this evening felt like old times. Peter Porter was to join them for supper. The wide damask-covered banquet table was elegantly set. Jane was overwhelmed with joy as she looked across the table and saw that she was surrounded with family and good friends. Trusted friends like Mr. Porter.

She noticed that her brother Cole was particularly handsome and groomed this evening. He wore his best dinner coat with matching purple cravat, and the family heirloom stick pin twinkled in the firelight. His hair was, for once, neatly combed in place.

He caught Jane staring at him.

"What ails you tonight, sister?" he whispered.

She smiled faintly. "Nothing ails me. I just wish mother and father could see you now. So sure of yourself, sitting at the head of the table among your family and important friends."

"Hush," he said gently as he carved the roast beef with steady hands and passed the plate to Miss Stiles. "I'll have no more flattery in this house. And if you must, cast your eyes at Henry. He is a changed young man." He nodded toward their little brother.

Jane laughed and focused on Henry. Cole was right. Henry looked as impressive as Cole, even his cowlick was fixed in place, laying flat atop his head. His brown breeches and jacket contrasted nicely with his freckles and fresh, clean look. It was a complete and miraculous transformation from the perpetually scruffy child of before. And his table manners had gone from zero to incredible. He no longer just reached without asking permission first. And it was all because of Emma Stiles. He had obviously surrendered to her charms.

Magic. Jane was convinced.

Emma sat beside Henry, in a high-neck gown of black taffeta with a single string of pearls hung around her neck. She sat firm and quiet, commanding a presence that seemed to draw the attention of all who sat at the table.

Jane had opted to dress moderately in a cotton dress of pale lavender, with pale pink ribbon belting her slender waist. In the gleam of soft candlelight and overhead chandelier, Jane Havens looked younger than her age and vulnerable.

The evening was gay but for one sour note. Hannah Browne. The older woman had not made peace with the new governess. She moved about to and from the table, arms loaded with plates and trays, but with a disgruntled expression. Her mood was not lost on Jane. She knew her too well. Jane did not know if Emma had noticed the hostile attitude. She had made no reference to it. Still, Jane remained fearful that Emma was indeed aware of the housekeeper's feelings. She was too perceptive a woman not to notice the disgruntled face each time the housekeeper served her.

"So, you're positive on how things are going, Cole?" Mr. Porter asked, dabbing the corner of his mouth lightly with the napkin.

"Yes, I believe so. We seem to be on solid footing for this time. The promise of a warm summer means we could do some work with the fields."

"Anything particular in mind?"

Cole drummed his fingers on the table. "Well, since the frost ruined so much, I thought I should lay in twice the amount of seed early, while the weather is ripe for it. There's no reason why we couldn't salvage enough crop by fall to justify our past losses. Do you think there's a chance that would work?"

Mr. Porter nodded slowly. "Don't see why that wouldn't work. And if it does, it will lighten next year's load—"

Jane was not paying attention to their dull talk of business and running a farm. She was watching Emma and Henry. While Hannah took away the roast beef and brought in dessert, Emma's slim, deft fingers had miraculously fashioned a damask napkin into the absolutely perfect shape of a snow white rabbit. Henry eyed it in total surprise and awe. He was attempting to get hold of Cole's and Mr. Porter's attention. Mr. Porter finally noticed and glanced across the table, breaking out in a wide smile.

"Well, well, look what we have here. Parlor tricks? Upon my soul, that is the most realistic rabbit I have ever seen." He turned to Emma. "Excellent, my dear."

Emma's hands stopped her work. Her cheeks flushed a deep pink.

"Oh, please forgive me. I was not aware we were being observed."

"Nonsense," Porter chuckled. "We were indulging in boring men's talk while you were doing something far more interesting." He turned to Henry. "What say you about that there rabbit, Henry?"

Henry's face lit up with a wide smile.

"Miss Stiles is the smartest girl ever. You should hear the bird calls she can make, and she sings prettier than any meadowlark I ever heard."

"Hush, now Henry," Emma said in a near whisper. "Do you seek to embarrass me with your flattery?"

Jane half expected Cole to break out with something not befitting the evening atmosphere, but she watched his smile widen as he admired the perfectly formed rabbit napkin.

"There seems to be more than one artist at Havenswood." His eyes traveled to Miss Stiles. "Outstanding work, Miss Stiles. Congratulations. Your rabbit is indeed a work of art."

Emma demurely lowered her head. "Thank you, Mr. Havens. It is nothing. A simple trick of folding and tucking only."

Jane beamed across the table at the governess. She was convinced that there was not a more exquisite woman born.

"Jane, my dear girl," Mr. Porter said, "I imagine that soon it shall be your turn to marry, have children and entertain them with things like this, I expect. With your beauty, certainly there are young men falling over themselves for your hand?" He looked at her with a teasing wink and smile.

Cole smirked while Jane sat back in her chair, taken by surprise.

"Give her time, Mr. Porter," Cole said. "Jane is still very young—"

"Now, now, my dear Miss Havens," Porter said hastily, "I did not intend to step on your sensibilities. I was only teasing, you understand. You will have ample time and plenty of choices before long."

"I can only hope," Cole added, a twinkle in his eyes. "If only my sister decides to want any of them."

Jane only stared down at her empty plate, feeling her cheeks flaming red hot. What must Emma be thinking? Why must the men discuss her in this fashion? Was she only an object with no say in her own affairs?

"I believe," Emma suddenly said quietly, "that Miss Havens is not unwise in her desire to wait. It is, after all, her prerogative as a woman and as a person."

Jane saw Cole's amusement fade and one eyebrow arch.

"Pray tell, Miss Stiles, what exactly is that supposed to mean?"

She gave the barest shrug of her shoulders, but Cole chose not to drop the question.

"Please, Miss Stiles, I'd like to hear what your views are on the subject."

She leveled her gaze at Cole.

"If you wish, Mr. Havens. A Havens woman, a woman of that stature, should be not only highly selective but patient and prudent." She shifted her icy blue eyes to

Jane, a slight smile tugging at her lips. "I believe Miss Havens certainly is all of those things. A woman of her beauty and station owes it to not only her family but to herself to choose the proper mate. I'm sure we all trust her to make the choices of her heart when the time comes."

She didn't say "husband." Jane stared at her, her eyes filled with gratitude and relief. Cole was rendered speechless. There was a brief silence. Emma Stiles had expressed her opinion in a succinct and pointed way. She had confidently told Jane and the others that she believed Jane was special.

Jane smiled and allowed that realization to spread like a warm fire through her and consume any doubts that Emma Stiles was a woman after her own heart.

***

That night, as Jane lay in her canopied bed, too filled with emotions to sleep, she thought about Emma Stiles. How fiercely she had defended her. A dizzying warmth filled Jane as she thought of the governess, sitting so exquisitely in the chair. She was certainly a spirited woman. When she spoke passionately, like she had that evening, her eyes became blue flames. And yet, she was so delicate—slender and courtly—so very beautiful. Jane allowed herself to dwell on fanciful thoughts of Emma, thoughts another woman should not indulge in about another woman. She couldn't help but wonder how soft Emma's lips would be to kiss.

Jane did not know when she finally drifted into deep sleep or when her wild and romantic longings subsided. She could not, in her wildest imaginings, know what great change was to dawn the next morning in her life.

***

In the bold, bright light of the following morning, Jane stopped by the kitchen to check with Hannah before deciding on her daily duties. She found the housekeeper washing crockery, her stout arms deep in a tub of sudsy water.

"Good morning, Hannah. Where has everyone got to? Havenswood's as quiet as a church on Saturday."

Hannah wiped her brow. "Well, seems like you overslept. Sleep too much and the morning goes on without you."

Jane laughed out loud. She was too refreshed and excited to take umbrage at Hannah's mood.

"My bed was too pleasant to leave it so early, you see. I only want a cup of coffee before I set out to check on Miss Stiles, Henry and Cole."

She took a peek through the gauzy curtains of the kitchen windows. The grass and the trees glowed a bright green and there was a golden haze that seemed to engulf the entire morning.

"Well, you missed Master Cole. He went to town to check on some bags of fertilizer that Mr. Porter arranged to be shipped for Havenswood. And both Henry and the governess left just a bit ago to fetch horses for a morning ride."

Jane's eyes widened in surprise. "Oh, I'd love to join them." She took a cup from the cupboard and moving quickly, filled it with coffee from the pot. "Why don't you like Miss Stiles, Hannah? I know how you feel, so don't deny it. But just having a feeling isn't enough to dislike someone."

"I have no reason to deny it," Mrs. Browne said, outraged. "I'm still entitled to my opinion around here, aren't I? I just don't get a good feeling in my gut about that one. She gives me the shivers, like when someone walks on my grave."

"Now that isn't fair, Hannah," Jane said patiently. "She's only just arrived and been here only a short time. You shouldn't be so standoffish with her."

Hannah frowned, looking at Jane carefully. "Has she said anything to you about me?"

"Of course she hasn't. She is too much of a lady."

Hannah Browne snorted. "She'd best not. I simply do not take a fancy to her, that's all. You excuse me, Miss Jane, but I don't like your Miss Stiles."

Jane took one final gulp of coffee. "I only wanted to understand your hesitation to welcome our guest, Hannah. And even though we don't agree, I would never limit your freedom of speech. It is your God-given right. If that's the way you feel."

Disturbed by Hannah's intense suspicions and dislike of Emma, but determined not to let the housekeeper's grim observations spoil the day, she nearly raced back to her room, changed into her riding clothes and took off to the stables.

Outside, the air was fresh and bracing. She quickly forgot all about the bad taste Hannah had left in her thoughts. Without even bothering to call for Gabe, Jane took her favorite black gelding, Shadow, and saddled him quickly herself.

As she rode off in a gallop, anxious to catch up with Emma and Henry, she saw Gabe in the distance, near the picket fence. He was mending broken plow blades. She rode astride, preferring that over the silly side saddle. Why should men have it easier? Emma's comments had emboldened her and taken root in her heart. She was indeed an independent woman and a Havens woman. She would do things her way.

At an easy trot and with a gentle application of the riding crop, the gelding steered toward Greenroad Woods, taking the worn, rutted country path leading from Havenswood. Jane spurred across the road at a gallop, entering the densest part of the woods where it began just beyond the west fields. The wind swept across here face, filling Jane with a sense of freedom and contentment.

The forest thickened, closely-knit branches growing more abundant and blocking out some of the sunlight. Jane slowed the gelding to a slower gait, allowing herself time to drink in the smell of the hemlock and maples. Nothing ever seemed to disturb the forest. It was forever timeless.

She found herself along the borders of Arrowhead Creek, a favorite bathing creek, on the way to Rock Lake, where she assumed Emma and Henry had gone, but she reigned in Shadow abruptly as she caught sight of her brother, all alone, near the center of the creek, jabbing at something in the water. Where was Emma? Jane looked around in a near panic. Why would Emma leave Henry all alone?

Her heart leapt to her throat. She brought Shadow to the grassy edge of the creek and dismounted.

"Henry Havens," she cried out, "you come back now."

She waved as she saw him stand and wave back with a big grin.

"Where is Miss Stiles?" Jane called out. Her words seemed to echo off the giant trees surrounding them.

Henry pointed over to the other side of the creek. In the distance, clear across the wide creek, Emma Stiles stood with her back to Jane and Henry, arms outstretched to a giant Oak. Its branches reached far into the sky. What was she doing? Why did she not respond?

Jane raised her voice. "Miss Stiles!" She yelled across the creek.

The governess did not respond. She stood, arms extended the length of her. Oblivious to Jane's call, she leaned her head back and stared at the heavens. Jane wondered how she could have gotten to that part of the creek, unless she'd taken the horse around the edge of the creek. But that wasn't heavily traveled land. It could not have been easy riding.

She had to round up Henry before worrying about Emma. She called back out to her little brother.

"You stay right there and don't move, Henry."

"Okay, Janey." He seemed very content to remain where he was, trying to catch frogs. Most boys would find that an ideal adventure. But Jane knew that the creek was deep in certain areas and she feared he might dip into one.

Jane mounted Shadow quickly and circled west, where the forest became thicker and offered less road. As she and the gelding worked their way to the other side of Arrowhead Creek, where Emma stood, Jane could hear a low, persistent chanting float through the woods. The words were coming from Emma, but Jane could not understand them. It wasn't English.

She finally came up beside Emma's horse, which was neatly tied to a narrow maple. Tying up her own horse, she dismounted and approached Emma. The governess's face was as serene as a marble statue. Her eyes were closed. She wore a riding skirt, white blouse and a black cincher. Her feather-covered hat lay at her feet and her exquisite black hair curled atop her head.

"Emma?" Jane spoke her name softly.

The other woman stopped chanting and looked directly at her. Her icy blue eyes were bright with a cold fire. She seemed disoriented, as if coming out of a trance.

Emma shook her head and then smiled at Jane.

"Jane, I did not hear you approach."

"What were you doing?" Jane asked, totally confused by what she had just seen and heard. "And why is Henry not being supervised more closely? He is virtually in the center of the creek. You probably don't know, but the creek has very deep sections. It isn't safe—"

"Come here, Jane," said Emma, raising an arm to beckon her.

Jane went to her obediently, not uttering another word about Henry. Emma took her hand and drew her close. Her voice was a whisper. A very intoxicating whisper in Jane's ears.

"Henry is fine. I would never put him in danger. You must believe that." She pulled Jane nearly into her arms. Jane did nothing to break away. She looked into the clear blue of Emma's eyes. They were positively hypnotizing. The governess smiled seductively at her.

"I want a special friendship with you, Jane. I do. I think you'd like that too..."

Jane shivered with a heat she had never felt before. Emma was gently rubbing her fingers along her face and Jane realized she did not want her to stop. What did she want?

Suddenly, Emma drew Jane into a tight embrace, their lips inches apart. Jane smelled the sweet breath from Emma's mouth.

"I know why you don't want a man, Jane Havens." Emma Stiles leaned in and kissed Jane. Softly at first, and then with more of a hunger.

Jane's thoughts exploded. She fully believed her heart had stopped and she would drop dead in this unbelievable woman's arms. All thought of Henry disappeared. There were only thoughts of Emma. Emma's lips. Emma's tongue. Her hands seared and practically branded Emma's body. Jane shuddered as their breasts touched. She wanted to evaporate into this woman.

When they parted, Jane felt that a part of her had been cut from her body. The warmth had been sucked from her breath. Emma held both of Jane's arms, gazing intently into her eyes.

"I have my own ways, dear Jane. I grew up in a forest, wild and without restraint. Please don't think me odd..." She studied Jane's face. "And please don't tell Cole or anyone else about all of this. This will be our secret and ours alone." She looked out to Henry.

Jane, still in a semi-stupor, followed Emma's gaze to her brother. His attentions were still focused on bugs, worms and toads. He remained innocent, having seen nothing of the shocking thing she had just done with another woman. For the briefest moment, Jane felt ashamed, but then a more fierce desire pushed those thoughts from her mind. Her heart and her body told her she wanted more. She wanted Emma Stiles's mouth upon hers again.

But Jane stood frozen, staring from Emma to Henry.

Emma put a hand softly on her shoulder. "Come, Jane, we should be getting back. It's close to dinner and I have a few lessons for Henry before the day's end." She smiled.

"You go on with Henry. I'll follow shortly," Jane said, her breath trembling.

"Very well, but don't be long," Emma said, leaning close again and brushing her lips gently over Jane's. "And remember our secret."

She turned and called to Henry to get back to the other side of the creek, grabbed her hat, and disappeared atop her horse. Jane was left with the strong feeling that Emma Stiles had just ridden off with her wildly beating heart.

She watched as her little brother took off running. He waded through waist high water and reached the other side with nary a wave her way. He had eyes only for Emma.

What kind of spell had this woman cast upon the Havens family?

Chapter 6

Suddenly, Havenswood had changed for Jane Havens. It surely was paradise.

For Jane, it was the home she now shared with Emma Stiles. She had never been happier. She'd requested Hannah bring forth the Napoleon brandy for supper. Her new found joy had not gone unnoticed by Cole. He saw the light in her eyes. And Henry was becoming the model of a little gentleman, thanks to Emma. Jane fervently blessed the day Mr. Porter had arrived bringing her into their lives.

She and Emma stood, side by side, at the entrance to the sitting room.

"Happy?" Emma asked, staring deeply into Jane's eyes.

"It feels like heaven. I feel so alive but am trying to understand...things."

"Yes, I don't wonder." The governess smiled. "Hush, now, here comes your brother."

Cole was approaching from the staircase, hands tucked into the waistband of his trousers. He wore a pleased smile. When he joined them, he bowed.

"Jane...Miss Stiles."

Jane couldn't suppress a giggle. Cole studied her carefully.

"If I didn't know better, dear sister, I would venture to guess you are smitten by a young man." He arched an eyebrow.

Jane cast a quick glance at Emma, who stood quiet. She knew they had to be careful.

"Well, you would be wrong on your guess, Cole. Can't a girl just be happy without a man somehow being involved?"

Cole looked over at Emma. "You see, Miss Stiles, how difficult my sister is on these matters. She will never be settled enough." He glanced back at Jane.

"I believe, Mr. Havens, that your sister is quite mature enough for anyone she chooses to give her attentions to when the time comes." She smiled at Cole and then at Jane. "Now, if you both will excuse me, I'll bid you both a good night."

Jane tried hard not to watch Emma.

"Goodnight, Em—uh, Miss Stiles."

Cole shot a look of surprise at her. His gaze followed the governess as she disappeared up the hallway and ascended the stairs. He turned back to Jane, shaking his head.

"Well, there have been quite a few changes around here, haven't there?"

"Cole, don't be upset. Emma is such a dear friend and we are near the same age and I so wanted a female companion. I just can't see her or treat her as a servant."

"Nevertheless, she is our servant," he said firmly. "You must remember your station and her place, Jane. It's improper and distasteful to befriend one's staff, no matter how dear they are to us. After all, it hasn't been that long since Miss Stiles arrived."

Jane sighed. "But she has meant and accomplished so much for us in such a short time, Cole. Just look at Henry for proof. He is so good now. Our little wild brother is well behaved that I almost don't recognize him. And you..." she paused, planning her words carefully. "I think your interest in painting has perked up, and it wouldn't surprise me to know you have actually begun to paint again. You're locked in your room all day, the way you used to do when you were painting." She smiled. "Have you begun to paint again?"

Cole's expression turned sour in an instant. "We are not discussing me or my painting, Jane. We were discussing Miss Stiles. Don't forget that you are a Havens, the Colonel's only daughter. My sister. Miss Stiles is merely our brother's governess. Part of the household staff. I merely want you to remember that."

Jane lowered her eyes. "Of course, Cole, I will," she said humbly.

"Very well, then." He appeared relieved that she'd offered no resistance. She grew frustrated at how often they squabbled over such things. She chose to remain close to Hannah, although the housekeeper's dislike of Emma was straining that relationship.

"Now, off to bed with you," he said. "That's where you should be."

She only nodded. This was not a good time or place to become obstinate with her brother over Emma. Jane only smiled and hugged him.

"Good night, Cole."

After reaching her room and closing the door behind her, she leaned her back against it, listening to Cole's boots step down the corridor to his own room. She still suspected he was indeed painting again and that pleased her. But there were so many more wondrous things to think and dream about, weren't there?

Jane could not sleep. Instead, she lay in her bed, counting moonbeams as they filtered through the portiere windows. She could not put the total meltdown she had experienced in the arms and kisses of Emma Stiles out of her head. What was the all-consuming fire that had raced through her body, leaving only smoldering embers needing more flame? Emma's lips had been sweet as honey and soft as the petals of a fresh, red rose. Was it a sin to feel this way for another woman? Would the Good Lord strike her down for desperately wanting the forbidden fruit Emma offered?

Just before she could no longer resist the sleep that she desperately needed, she realized that her heart had already seized on the truth. She was falling in love with Emma Stiles. Their governess. An employee. A woman. She would not fight it and she would fight Cole to win her right to love whomever she wanted. All she could do now was hope that Emma also loved her.

Jane Havens took her thoughts into a deep, contented sleep.

***

The following day began with a surprise, and not one Jane found comforting. She nearly had to drag it from Hannah's lips that Miss Stiles had once again taken Henry to Arrowhead Creek to bathe before lessons. At first, it seemed like a fine idea if Emma thought it healthy and helping Henry, but then a deep and troubling disappointment set in. Why had Emma not invited her or even mentioned it the night before? Did she not want her company? Did she not feel the same way? Had their passionate kisses meant nothing? Were they just part of a game she was not privy to?

Jane furiously wished she'd gone along. She wanted to be near Emma. She wanted to feel the heat upon her skin. The weather was heavy and humid. Her clinging undergarments told her that summer was inching ever closer with each morning.

Cole was locked in his room and Jane had set today to spend time with the wisteria. They were already in need of serious trimming. If Emma had left her behind, the wisterias certainly were welcoming to her. They were in full bloom, with splashes of purple, white and blue. She spent nearly an hour watering all of them from the sprinkler can she used especially for her wisteria.

When the morning wore on and the sun finally became too hot for her, she found refuge in the veranda. Jane sighed as she removed the sun hat and wiped her brow. There was an ache in her heart that she knew was from missing and wondering about Emma. It was all so confusing. Was this what love felt like?

She sat down in one of the cane chairs, her slender frame enclosed by the fan-like contours of the chair. She loved to sit there and daydream. The peaceful hours of the morning were her favorite time. The front lawn seemed to have come alive overnight. It was a bright and shimmering green. Or maybe everything just seemed to be more alive because she was more alive and could suddenly see the beauty around her. Yes, summer was coming and love and enchantment seemed to fill the air.

But her idyllic morning abruptly changed in an instant. The fierce, rattling squeal of buggy wheels on the roadway and loud snorting of horses broke her peaceful contemplations. The sound of a man's voice she did not recognize sent Jane racing from her fantasies. Her heart beat at an alarming rate.

Approaching madly into the cobble stoned perimeter in front of Havenswood was a small black buggy. It drew to a sudden halt, rocking on its springs as two large black horses pawed to a stop.

Something was wrong.

Jane straightened, her eyes wide in shock. A tall, lanky stranger alighted from the buggy in haste, his clothes soaking wet. In his arms, he carried a figure. Jane caught her breath. It was Henry and he too was equally drenched! He was partially wrapped in a woolen blanket. Behind the stranger carrying Henry, ran Emma Stiles. Beautiful and frightened Emma, her face pale with fear. The tall man with her little brother ran quickly to the portico at full speed. Emma tried valiantly to keep up with him despite the bustled skirt that tangled around her feet. As they walked briskly by Jane into the house, the governess looked forlorn. Her clothes were decidedly damp. They disappeared into the house.

Her mouth dry and her heart at her throat, Jane rushed after them. They had completely missed her sitting in the fan shaped chair and she'd been too shocked to call after them.

It was pure pandemonium inside Havenswood. Jane followed the clatter of commotion and raised voices to the living room where Henry had been taken. She dashed into the room, praying her little brother be safe, only to find that the tall stranger had propped him up in the Colonel's favorite lounge chair and swung the chair around to face the open fire place. But where was Emma? Jane searched the room but she was missing.

Jane burst toward Henry. He sat up straight, huddled tightly in his blanket, cowlick plastered down on his still wet hair. His eyes glittered with fear. The stranger knelt over him, studying his face intently.

"Janey—" Henry called out when he saw her, attempting a smile.

"Henry, sweetheart," Jane said. "Oh, dear brother, what on earth happened to you? I was so worried when I saw them carry you in. Are you all right?"

"He'll be fine, miss. Nothing to be alarmed about," the stranger said stepping aside for Jane. "Our young fellow here took a bit of a ducking."

"A ducking?" Jane blurted. "What do you mean?" She looked at Henry. "Dear boy, what happened? Won't you tell Janey?"

"I...got wet, that's all," he said morosely and stared away into the fire.

"Is that all? Hannah had said you and Miss Stiles went for a swim, but—"

The tall man laughed until Jane's angry stare cut it short. "I see nothing humorous about this, sir," she said.

"My apologies, miss. I should explain and also introduce myself. I'm Doctor Richard Rydell. It was fortunate that I was passing by Arrowhead Creek when I came upon this young chap who appeared to be having a bit of a difficulty in the deeper part of the creek. I merely gave him a hand and pulled him out. So, other than a ducking and a total scare, Henry here will be quite all right. I've instructed your governess, Miss Stiles, to keep the fireplace going. Several hot toddies and Henry will be his old self again. That's all there is to it, really."

Jane ignored the doctor.

"But Henry, you were going bathing. How did you end up in the water with all your clothes on?" Thoughts of Emma on the other side of the creek, and what happened between them, came rushing forth. It was near impossible to push those thoughts away.

Dr. Rydell answered. "Apparently, as he told me the story, he ventured out along the bough of a sycamore which extended over the deep end of the creek. He said something about finding a swallow's nest. I wouldn't mind it too much, my dear lady. The worst is over and done with. I'm only too glad I was there to help."

Jane finally got her wits about her. "Please forgive me, doctor, I have forgotten my manners. I am in your debt for bringing my little brother back to me safe and sound. If anything had happened to Henry, I—" She stared down at him. For once, he avoided looking her in the eyes. It was not often that he did that. He was ashamed and afraid. But who was he afraid of? Cole? He knew she would never punish or berate him.

"I'm really sorry, Janey," he finally said. "I was just trying to fetch a swallow's egg for Miss Stiles. She loves birds. I wanted to surprise her—"

"Oh, I imagine she was very surprised," Jane sighed. "Surprised out of her wits I imagine."

"And that is putting it mildly."

It was Emma, from somewhere behind. Jane turned around to face her. Emma's face was still pale, drained of all color. She wanted to reach out to her, to hold her close, and to warm her with the fires of their love.

"You mustn't take the guilt upon your back alone. These things happen with children," Jane said softly.

"Indeed, but not when they are with their governess. I should have kept him in sight. I..." She paused, casting her gaze away and staring at the fire.

"To her benefit," Dr. Rydell said, "This fine lady's screams drew me to the creek. She should share your gratitude for saving this boy's life. If not for her calling out, he might not be quite so ready for another go."

"I should see about the fireplace," Emma said quietly, shrugging off Dr. Rydell's praise. She swept past Jane and Dr. Rydell and went to the hearth, crouching to kindle the dead logs. Henry sniffled loudly and Dr. Rydell leaned over him once again, hand on his forehead.

"Don't you go getting sick, young man. You'll have no fun if you do. Summer will be here and I know you won't want to greet it in bed, would you?"

"No, sir, you're right about that."

"How old are you, Henry?"

"Twelve."

Dr. Rydell laughed. "Well then, Henry, I forbid you to get sick."

"Dr. Rydell," Jane interrupted, "How can we repay you for your services? Surely, there must be a fee—"

Exactly at that moment, Cole came into the room, eyes alarmed. Before he could even ask a question, Emma began to apprise him of what had happened. She did so with rare courage, admitting her mistakes and carelessness, and taking full responsibility and blame. Jane glowed with admiration for her. She could not suppress a slight smile. The expression on Cole's face did not change. His mood surprised her. She almost feared the backlash and anger that would befall Emma, but in the end, he merely shook his head slowly.

"Don't be so willing to accuse yourself of wrongdoing, Miss Stiles. The vicissitudes of this life are only too familiar to me. Henry's safe and that is all that really matters. I only ask that you reconsider all outdoor excursions in the future unless you are able to watch him at all times. I do not expect you to run to keep up with him." Emma nodded politely and Cole turned to Dr. Rydell, regarding him with approval.

"And you, Dr. Rydell, have my deepest thanks and gratitude. I must confess, kind sir, to not knowing you or hearing of you in town. I pride myself in being familiar with most of Havens Falls' inhabitants. Are you newly moved here?"

"Indeed. I just set up my practice in Havens Falls. And it is a great pleasure. You see, Mr. Peter Porter is a dear old friend of my family. He and my late father were friends before my family moved to New York."

Cole smiled and looked very pleased. "Well, what good luck. Mr. Porter is our solicitor and a personal friend. A good man indeed."

Jane smiled as the two men sealed their approval with a handshake, but wondered as she noticed Emma stiffen visibly when Dr. Rydell mentioned New York.

"Mr. Porter is a good old timer," Rydell said. I hope to use him as my welcoming committee for the town's board of directors. I wish to be fully involved in the community, Mr. Havens, and will most assuredly need all the influential assistance I can get. It isn't easy to set up a medical practice in a small town. The oldsters will be suspicious of me until I prove my worth or deliver my first baby or mend my first broken bone."

"Or save Henry Havens from drowning," Cole chuckled. "I should say you've begun your career quite brilliantly in Havens Falls."

The doctor shook his head and smiled. "Oh, but you would have done the same, Mr. Havens."

"May we offer you a drink, Dr. Rydell?" Cole stepped toward the brandy bottle in the corner.

"No, thank you, Mr. Havens. These two lovely ladies have given me sufficient compensation and gratitude." He bowed toward the women, his eyes lingering longer on Emma.

Cole stopped in mid-step. Jane noticed how disappointed her brother was in not being able to have the excuse for a drink.

"I say, Dr. Rydell, did you know that our governess here, Miss Stiles, also hails from New York?"

"Well, does she now," the doctor said, his gaze steady on Emma. "Small world. As a matter of fact, I was struck by the notion that I had encountered Miss Stiles before today. What part of New York do you hale from, Miss Stiles, if I may ask? I have lived off Washington Square Park for years. I wonder if that's why your face is so familiar to me. Perhaps—"

"No, doctor," Emma said quickly, her back to the crackling blaze in the fireplace. "I think not. My family...my mother and I lived far from your New York. We have never met. I am sure of that."

Dr. Rydell studied her closely. "Still, I would almost vouch for having met you."

Emma shook her head. "No," she smiled sweetly. "And I'm afraid that I have no recollection of you whatsoever."

"Well, doctor," Cole interrupted, "I feel I must at least invite you to dinner in turn for saving our Henry's life. I do hope you will accept the invitation?"

Richard Rydell seemed to weigh the offer. He was considering Emma Stiles. Finally, he smiled at Cole.

"I should be delighted, Mr. Havens."

"Done, then. Shall we say Friday evening? Eight o'clock? I can promise that our Mrs. Browne will be preparing something special, and I assure you that she is the best cook in all of Pennsylvania proper."

Dr. Rydell bowed and nodded. "It would be an honor. But now, I must take my leave."

Emma quickly moved toward him. "I'll escort you to your carriage, Dr. Rydell."

"Of course, Miss Stiles."

Suddenly, Henry, who'd been sitting quietly and intently looking at the burning fire, sat up.

"Goodbye, Dr. Rydell. You sure are a good swimmer."

Rydell smiled back at him. "I spent lots of time in swimming holes when I was your age. I shall have to teach you new strokes if I might be permitted."

Henry's eyes opened wide. "I should like that very much."

"Well—" Rydell looked at Cole.

"Oh, I think we can discuss that on Friday after dinner," Cole said, ruffling the top of Henry's head.

Dr. Rydell tipped his head. "Good day to you, then, Miss Havens and to you, Mr. Havens." He followed Emma out of the living room.

Cole had already poured himself a drink before the front door closed, a look of speculation in his eyes.

"What are you thinking, Cole?" Jane asked.

"Did you notice his clothes? Well cut. Those aren't Simpson Street clothes on his back. He must have a bit of money already. I don't wonder of course..." He took a swallow. "Medicine can be quite lucrative. But I do wonder why or what would make him move a sound practice from New York to come here to Havens Falls? There is not much wealth in Havens Falls."

"I'm certain he has his reasons."

"Oh, I'm sure he does," Cole agreed, "but that is my point, dear sister. What are those reasons? Why come to such a small town?"

"Well, he's a good doctor," Henry piped up. "I feel better already."

"You are nothing but a young savage," Cole laughed, pointing a finger at his little brother. "All you know anything about is getting in trouble."

Jane sat by Henry's side, stroking his forehead. "Dr. Rydell does seem like a man who knows his business. If he's here, it's because he believes he is needed."

"True enough, sister. I concur," Cole acknowledged. "Perhaps he doesn't need the money, and there is certainly plenty of work to be had here. Any friend of Mr. Porter's is obviously a fine man. We shall see." He turned to Henry. "But you, little brother, must be more careful," he said sternly.

"Aw, Cole—" Henry looked away into the fire, but Cole came around and blocked his view. He smiled down at him.

"I'm proud of you for trying to do something nice for Miss Stiles, but do be careful. Please."

Henry rubbed his eyes in disbelief. "You aren't angry with me?"

"No, I am not. Nor am I angry with Miss Stiles. I am actually quite pleased that you've grown to like her so much. She's certainly had a very positive effect on you, and we can all see the results of her tutelage. This affair is done. We shall speak no more of it."

Henry smiled wide. "That's sure a relief. Gosh, I was sure you'd break a glass or two." He turned to Jane. "You heard that, Janey? Cole says everything is okay."

"Of course he does," she said, taking her little brother's hand and squeezing.

"Well," Cole said, "I'll be going back to my room. I certainly hope this is the end of all the excitement for today." He looked at Henry. "Mind you, follow the doctor's orders and keep warm."

As Cole left the room, Jane heard the wheels of Dr. Rydell's buggy drive off.

"He's nice, Janey. Isn't Dr. Rydell nice? Can I show him the painting Cole did of me when he comes to dinner on Friday?"

"Of course, dearest."

Emma glided into the living room, curiously quiet and subdued. There was a faint flush to her cheeks. What could that mean, Jane wondered. Had something transpired between Emma and Dr. Rydell?

"Did the doctor get off all right?" she asked, curious about Emma's mood.

"Yes, he's gone."

Jane had to know what was going on with the woman who had passionately kissed her in the forest. That had to have meant something.

"He seems an interesting man, don't you think? Do you suppose he is a good doctor?"

Emma walked towards her. "I couldn't say, Jane."

As Emma came to stand very close behind her, Jane felt the heat rise inside her. And it wasn't the fire in the hearth. She checked her younger brother. Henry was completely occupied with the dancing of the tall flames burning in the fireplace.

"Cole liked him, too," Jane continued. "Did you notice?" It was all she could babble as she tried to settle the butterflies aflutter in her belly.

Emma leaned in closer behind her, close enough that Jane could feel the beat of the other woman's heart on her back and the push of her breasts.

Emma pressed her lips to Jane's ear, the moistness hot upon her skin.

"Jane Havens, I have no interest in that man or any other man," she murmured. "There is only you."

Chapter 7

Sleep was not a luxury Jane was afforded that night. After Henry was put to bed, she never saw Emma again. Lying in bed, the silvery moon bright in the sky, her thoughts were unsettled. Emma Stiles had brought unbridled joy and something far more to her but she had also brought doubt.

Outside, it was a quiet night, making Havenswood's creaks and settling sounds seem louder and more intrusive. But the light knock on her door was very distinct.

Jane sat up, alarmed. Who could it be at such a late hour? She reached for her robe and tip toed to the door to make sure it had actually been a knock. Rap, rap, rap. The soft knock came again, more insistent.

"Who is it?" Jane whispered, her face to the cool wood of the door.

"Emma."

Without hesitation, Jane opened the door.

Emma, dressed in a pale blue robe, a satin ribbon tying it at the waist, rushed swiftly inside the room.

"Emma, is there anything wrong? How is Henry?" Jane asked as she closed the door and locked it.

"Nothing is wrong, dear Jane." Emma came to her side and took both her hands in hers. "I could not sleep and hoped you would not think me mad if I invited you to a moonlight walk in the garden." There was a strange, wild fire in her crystal blue gaze.

"It's so late—"

"Please say you will, Jane. The night is lovely and still young..." She paused, softly brushing Jane's cheeks. "Lovely like you. Come, Jane, we can talk. Don't you wish to spend time alone, together? She drew her closer.

Jane's thoughts always got muddled when Emma was so close. She could feel the heat between them. She knew it would be hopeless to deny Emma anything. And why not take all the joy and freedom being with Emma gave her? Who was it that made such silly rules about proper etiquette on when one should be in bed? Alone and miserable.

Emma brushed a light kiss on Jane's lips.

"Shall we go?"

"In our robes?" Jane asked, looking down at her own light robe.

"Yes, of course. It is warm and the air is filled with marvelous scents and sounds."

She pulled Jane towards the door. "Grab your shoes and let's go quietly so as not to wake the others or Goldy. She will bark and wake every soul in the house."

The both walked carefully on their tip toes through the hall and down the staircase, Jane trying valiantly to suppress a giggle. The thrill in her chest was like an aphrodisiac, her head giddy from the excitement.

Once outside, the gust of the warm yet damp breeze lifted their flimsy robes and tousled their loose hair. Emma's wild black mane blew like the long feathers of a raven in the starlit night.

Walking hand in hand outside in her garden, in the evening, with Emma, Jane couldn't fathom or explain what she felt. The exhilaration, the complete and wild abandon was like magic. She glanced back at Havenswood. All was quiet and dark. All were asleep in their beds. Only she and Emma were awake, and that felt intoxicating. Jane suddenly thought of Hannah, even though she couldn't figure out why. The housekeeper would give her a tongue lashing if she caught her out here with the woman she called "dark."

Emma suddenly drew her closer and tucked Jane's arm through her own as they continued to walk quietly along the white-painted stones of Havenswood garden.

"Emma," Jane asked softly, "What is it that kept you awake tonight? Are you worried about Henry?"

It took a moment for the other woman to answer. Jane feared she would not.

"No, Jane, Henry will be fine." That was all she said.

Then Jane feared it might be Hannah and her rude behavior toward the governess.

"Is it any problem with the household staff? Hannah? I've spoken to her about her brusque manner." It was the most polite way of putting it to Emma.

Emma only smiled a quiet smile. "No, you must not worry about that. Your Mrs. Browne is just old enough to worry about new intrusions."

"New intrusions?"

"Yes. She feels her position threatened. I've never even spoken to her much, yet she feels I am a threat to her. I had decided to make a concentrated effort to convince her that I mean her no harm."

"She really is a dear," Jane said eagerly. "She's been with our family all her life. I am none too pleased with her resentment of you when you have done nothing to deserve it. I truly hoped she'd be sensible."

Emma laughed, a sweet sound enveloped and swept away by the evening breeze. "Let us please forget Hannah Browne tonight, Jane."

They had walked deep into the garden, among the wisteria. Emma guided Jane toward a tall wisteria tree, furthest away from the main garden.

"Here, Jane, let us sit under your favorite tree."

It was one of the largest of the wisteria and dressed with blooms of such deep purple that they blended into the shade of nightfall. The two women were nearly hidden from sight.

"Let's sit down," Emma said, pulling Jane to the soft grass.

"But we have no blanket," Jane protested. "The grass will be wet and chilled."

"Nonsense. Don't fuss, Jane. Here..."

Without hesitating, Emma removed her robe, revealing only a night shirt underneath and nothing else.

Jane tried to stop her. "Oh no, Emma. You'll catch a cold."

But the other woman just shook her head and spread out her beautiful robe on the grass.

"For my lovely Jane, a place to rest." She pointed for Jane to sit. "You should know that I pranced about the woods of New York with far less on my back, dear."

Emma sat down so close to Jane that she was nearly on her lap. Jane was only too aware of the extreme warmth radiating from her.

For God's sake, she has only the flimsy sleep shirt on her!

Emma took Jane's hands and clutched them to her bosom, her blue eyes gazing deep into Jane's

"You know, dearest, how important it is that we keep our secret from the others. You know we must."

"It's unfair, I think," Jane said. "We are all God's children."

"Your purity of innocence is your beauty, sweet Jane. If only the civilized world believed so absolutely in the equality of human beings and women too."

"I will never speak our secret, Emma. You needn't worry about me."

Emma's smile faded. "You say that now, Jane, but what about later, when life may become more difficult? There is something fragile I must reveal to you right now if we intend to cultivate our relationship so that it becomes magnificent, like this flowering wisteria. I insist on transparency between us."

"What do you speak of?" Jane asked.

Emma leaned into Jane and kissed her softly on the lips—A lingering kiss that sent Jane's entire body into a slowly growing fire.

A light wind whispered through the wisteria, sending the flowers dancing and swaying and cooling Jane's blazing cheeks.

"Jane, only you must learn the truth. I can trust it with no one else, less I should be thrust out of Havenswood and society forever. I would be a homeless outcast...again."

Jane stared at her, surprised and confused.

"Again? What is so horrible that you would be judged unsuitable for society? Oh, Emma, you know you can trust me implicitly. I would never, ever hurt you."

Emma smiled wistfully, her eyes with a distant, faraway look.

"I have come a long way to learn how to trust again, Jane. It is still quite difficult to discern those who are worthy of that trust. But I feel you are special."

"And you are like a radiant, regal queen, Emma Stiles."

At this, Emma laughed out loud, putting her hand quickly to her lips to muffle her laughter.

"Perhaps you will think differently of me after I tell you what I must," she said seriously, eyes steadily watching Jane.

"My dear, we are worlds apart yet, here we are. I want to personally apologize for not being as vigilante with Henry as I should have been at the creek. When I am out there, among the trees, lakes and all the creatures of nature, my past life comes alive. It becomes my present. I sometimes forget where I am."

Jane studied Emma's face closely. "What are you trying to say to me? I don't understand. You speak in riddles, like Cole."

Emma shook her head. "I am not Cole. I don't want to be like anyone else in your world. There must be only you and me." She once again took Jane's hands. "Promise me. You and me only."

There was a fire in her eyes, a blaze that sparkled blue under the moonlight.

"I promise, Emma." There was no Henry and no Cole in Jane's thoughts and she felt no guilt.

"Jane, my mother...my mother and I lived in poverty. We lived in a very shabby, tiny house made of logs and old wooden planks in the woods, not far from New York City. We had nothing but the few old clothes on our backs, and ate whatever food we could gather from the woods or saved from well-meaning folks in the city..." She paused, her eyes growing wilder.

"Jane, do you have any idea what living like that means? Do you have any idea what the pain of hunger is really like? When the only meal on your plate is a few berries from the trees outside and a hard piece of week old bread? Do you know the pain inside your gut that feels like claws are ripping your insides? Do you, Jane?" Her voice was an angry whisper.

"Emma, no, please, don't be so upset." She tried to calm her by squeezing and rubbing the other woman's hands. "I've never known those things you speak of. But I am here for you now. I'm listening. I...love you, Emma. I love you."

Emma stared at her, the wild look in her eyes subsiding, a smile tugging at her lips.

"You don't even know who you say you love, do you, sweet Jane. Do you know me?"

"I know enough. I know what you've let me see."

"Oh, but there is more. So much more. But I warn you, do not forsake me by the time I finish. Do not think me a monster not worthy of you, or Henry, or my job."

"I shan't, dear Emma. I shan't."

Emma cast her gaze to the sky.

"A hungry human being will do just about anything for food, Jane. Anything." She leveled her gaze at Jane.

Jane inhaled, an ugly thought crossing her mind. "Emma, you never...you never—"

"No, Jane, I never did harm to a living soul. I never killed, if those are your fears. But I comforted killers and those with sins blackening their souls. I made them clean to be able to enter their precious Heaven and meet their cruel lord."

Jane's heart was beating too hard. The words Emma was saying were disturbing, bordering on blasphemous.

"Emma, please stop it. I don't understand."

Emma took a tight hold of both of Jane's shoulders. "Jane, do you know what a sin eater is? Do you?"

"No, I don't know. I don't know." Jane was becoming increasingly uncomfortable.

Emma's eyes became glassy as she intently stared at Jane. "I ate sins, Jane! I ate the sins of those that died with their sins intact, condemned by the Christian lord to a lake of fire if not cleansed. The unforgiven. Those wanting to knock upon the door of Heaven and be permitted entry. Do you understand what I did, Jane? What I did while my mother sat in that shabby house starving? I sat beside a rotting body and ate bread and drank wine atop that corpse. By consuming the food on the dead, I consumed their sins. My soul became the receptacle for every foul act and sin committed by the deceased. And for that, I was paid with good food and sometimes with coin. We could eat then, my mother and I, until there was no more food or coin to buy it and then I would go out and eat more sin."

She stopped, spent of energy, her shoulders sagging, but her eyes still upon Jane. "You see, my Jane, my soul is blacker than black to your God and quite worthless." She laughed without mirth.

Jane grabbed her fiercely and held Emma's slender frame tight. The initial shock and revulsion of what she'd heard was replaced by an overwhelming love and need to comfort her with her love.

"Oh, dear Lord, my darling Emma."

Suddenly, Emma withdrew from her embrace and glared at Jane, a fierce, haunted look in her icy blue eyes.

"Your Lord? In your Lord's eyes, I have consumed so many sins, I am condemned to the fires of hell for eternity. There will be no one to eat all the sins I have in my soul."

She laughed a wild, nervous laugh. "It is a good thing your Lord means nothing to me. I worship, I gain power and strength from the gods of nature. There is beauty and forgiveness and acceptance in nature."

Jane was shocked and appalled at what Emma had said.

"Oh, please, stop it, Emma. None of that is true! The Lord accepts and forgives all the sins of those who come to him. I know nothing about what you have spoken, but no one can take another's sin from them. Only God can forgive and wipe clean sin."

"Don't you understand, Jane? Your lord forsook me and my mother when I was forced to do what I had to do. And then my mother was taken from me in a cruel manner indeed. No, your God has no meaning in my life."

"No!" Jane made to get up. "I won't listen to you speak this blasphemy." She looked Emma deep in the eyes as she felt her own begin to water. "I love you too much to allow you to lose your soul."

"Please, Jane, don't forsake me too." Emma held her down and pulled her into a tight embrace. They held each other close, both kneeling on the now dew-wet robe.

"Dear Emma, my promises to you are real, but you mustn't allow all that rage to consume you...us." She ran a finger along Emma's cheek.

"But I need and want you to know me completely, Jane. Only by knowing me can you truly love me."

Emma kissed Jane's waiting lips hungrily, gently forcing her tongue into Jane's soft, moist mouth. Jane pressed her body even tighter into Emma. She knew she could no longer control the flames of desire that were blazing through her insides.

Emma's kisses began to move down Jane's neck, her tongue leaving a hot, wet streak. When Emma began to slip Jane's robe off, Jane shivered and inhaled.

"Out here?" She whispered hoarsely into Emma's ear.

"The perfect temple for our love," Emma said, swiftly flinging the robe aside.

Jane's body trembled with unbridled desire.

"Darling," Emma said, pausing. "You tremble like a falling leaf. Is it too cold?"

"No," Jane breathed. "Please, don't stop. I can't." She kissed Emma hard, urging her hands as she lifted the nightgown over her head.

Naked under her beloved wisteria tree, Jane Havens felt no cold, no shame only fire. Fire and heat and lust for Emma Stiles. The throbbing between her legs was nearly impossible to bear without moaning out loud.

Emma removed her night shirt and knelt fully exposed before Jane. Jane's gaze devoured every part and curve of her body. The darkness between her legs was as raven as the wild hair atop her head. An inky dark triangle amidst pale thighs.

Jane bent to put her mouth on the nipples that stood erect and ready for her, but Emma stopped her. She kissed Jane softly. "Close your eyes, Jane. I brought something special."

Jane would have done whatever Emma wanted. She needed her desperately.

"I trust you." She closed her eyes tight, intent to not peek. No, she would never peek. There was no going back now. She was completely in Emma Stiles's power. Another sweet breeze brushed across Jane's body, sending tingles of desire through her.

"Open your eyes, darling."

Emma held a small bottle of a dark, golden liquid before her, smiling wide.

"We don't need alcohol, do we?" Jane didn't want to think of Cole and his abuse of it. She wanted no part of that addiction.

"It isn't alcohol, Jane, it's a secret oil. A delight that will open your senses and take you to an ecstasy you never dreamed of." Her gaze took in every part of Jane. She took the small cork and threw it on the grass, putting a drop of the liquid on her finger and applying it behind each of Jane's ears and then her wrists. It was a strong, heady scent that smelled of heat, not sweet but not unpleasant.

"What is that?"

Emma applied the oil to the spots on herself. "It's called Patchouli oil. It's an aphrodisiac, an oil used for centuries to inspire artists and drive lovers wild. I learned how to make it myself with plants." She put the stopper back on the bottle. "Inhale, Jane. Drink up the scent with your nostrils. Feel the heat with your body."

Jane closed her eyes and breathed deeply. An overwhelming ache coursed from between her legs straight up to her heart. She felt herself woozy and intoxicated with the scent of the oil and the flames of desire imploding within her. She opened her eyes to see if it was having the same effect on Emma.

Emma smiled coyly at Jane and began to fondle herself, touching her breasts, sliding her hands to the blackness between her thighs and slipping her finger inside.

Jane screamed, unable to keep her hunger under control, but Emma stopped her scream with a finger to her lips.

"Hush, hush." She then grabbed Jane again and softly laid her back on the robe, lying atop her. She plunged her finger into Jane's abundant auburn curls. "Now, my darling Jane, we shall truly have a secret to keep."

She proceeded to lick her way down Jane's body as Jane arched herself into Emma. Jane didn't know if it was the oil, but her body felt like an inferno of desire. As Emma placed her knee between Jane's legs and parted them, moved her mouth to the place between, Jane could no longer control the loud moan that left her lips.

No one heard the sounds of ecstasy coming from under the blooming, swaying large wisteria tree.

**

Of course, there had been no sleep for Jane that night, only thoughts of Emma and the feel of Emma possessing her, body and soul. The volcano inside of her was still active and spilling forth hot lava. She needed Emma. It had been an epiphanic moment in Jane's life. In some ways, it had rendered her nice, comfortable notions about love, society, mores and her faith open for questions. What all these new revelations might do to her orderly world, she could not guess and frankly, Jane didn't feel the desire to contemplate those deep thoughts this morning.

Jane strongly felt that the sooner she had her conversation with Cole, the better. Especially now. As much as she wanted to be with Emma again, Jane knew the governess was tutoring Henry in his room at least for today until he felt better. The last thing she wanted was to overwhelm Emma with her constant need to be with her.

So Jane went in search of Cole. Havenswood felt sunny, bright and even more wonderfully alive than ever before. Jane knew why. She found Cole in the skylight room. It was the perfect room for an artist, whether a painter or a poet. It was a large and open space, where the light found each corner and bathed everything in a soft brightness. The Colonel had used it as a reading and recreation room, but Cole had claimed it as the perfect place to create art.

And he was painting again, as Jane suspected he would. The room was mostly empty but for two large easels, scattered canvases, brushes and tubes of paint. There was also an over-sized mahogany desk littered with sheets of paper, ink bottles and quill pens.

"Oh, hello, Jane," he said absent-mindedly, as he continued studying his drawing board. He wore his old, stained shirt he favored for painting, sleeves rolled above his elbows. Jane peeked over his shoulders.

He was working on a beautiful pastoral scene that to Jane, appeared to be the area behind Havenswood, approaching Greenroad Woods. She noted with joy that he had charcoaled the outlines of her wisteria, some of the purple already painted in. The wisteria where she and Emma had made love.

"Cole, how pretty that is."

"What?" He looked at the painting. "Oh, sure, yes. I started the sketch a few days ago. It's a scene out back, with the garden. You know, the colors out there are vibrant. In oils, they will shine."

"I'm so happy, Cole."

"Happy, Jane? About what?"

"That you're painting, of course," she said, not wanting to mix her own reason for bursting happiness with Cole.

"Of course," he growled at her in mock gruffness. He inhaled deeply and exhaled. "It feels good to paint again, Jane, to dream again. And I've actually scribbled several lines of a poem." He eyed her carefully.

"You seem to glow, dear sister. I might just make you my next subject." He smiled and raised an eyebrow. "Is there someone or something special going on that you haven't told your big brother about? You know I will need to approve of everything and everyone." He kept his gaze on her.

Jane suddenly thought this was not the best moment to approach Cole about Emma and their friendship.

Dear Lord, don't let him see my flushed cheeks!

She smiled and took his hand. "I'm just overjoyed to see you so alive and painting again in this room."

He eyed her for a moment more, then turned back to his drawing. "I'm glad to be back, dear sister. Your wisteria shall be the centerpiece of the painting."

***

Just before suppertime, Henry popped into Jane's room. She had not seen Emma the whole day and was desperate to see her at dinner.

Jane had spent her afternoon lazing through some of her mother's treasures—lockets, cameos and the family album. The past had suddenly become a strong pull.

Her mother had stored all of her delicate, hand-woven, expensive garments in a large cedar trunk, saving them for Jane to inherit at the time of betrothal. Undergarments and sheer gowns were wrapped in soft tissue paper. They were old, of course, but that did not take away their beauty. They were supremely elegant and feminine. These were the only treasures of finery that Jane truly owned.

Sadness suddenly gripped her. She complained so often of her lack of new and expensive things, while never even realizing the horrors Emma and others like her experienced throughout their lives. Emma had never had fine things. Never.

Jane had to brush those horrifying images of what Emma revealed that night from her mind. It was terrifying way to live and Jane hoped and prayed that Emma would never have to live that way again.

That's when Henry thankfully broke her train of thought. Her beloved little brother, bright-eyed and glowing, held a newspaper cut-out in his hand, fashioned in the shape of a Christmas tree.

"Janey, look. Ain't it pretty?"

"*Isn't* it pretty, Henry," she corrected him. Jane eyed the cleverly fashioned pattern. "Oh, that is ever so fancy and perfect." She noticed that someone, probably Emma, had written *Merry Christmas* across the paper. "Did Miss Stiles do that for you?"

His eyebrows furrowed in displeasure. He took back his prized paper tree.

"I did it, Janey. Me. Not Miss Stiles." His scowl softened. "Of course, Miss Stiles did show me how to make it and signed it for me, but I did this all on my own."

Jane looked at him fondly. This surely could not be the young hellion who had ridden roughshod over the entire household only months before. It did not seem possible that Emma could work such powerful magic in such a short time. She had converted Henry Havens into a proper, well-behaved child.

"You do like her, don't you Henry?"

"Like who?" He swirled the newspaper tree in his hand, avoiding her gaze and question.

"Why, Miss Stiles, silly."

"Oh, well, I guess she's all right. She sure is a good teacher. Who would've thought anyone could get me to like arithmetic, right Janey?"

Jane laughed. "It certainly wouldn't hurt you to at least learn to do sums."

"I guess not. That's what she says. Anyway, yeah, she's all right."

It was so important for both Henry and Cole to like Emma. They just had to.

"I'm glad you like her, Henry. And I'm also glad to see you feeling like yourself again. Now, off you go. I have to clean up and dress for suppertime. Did you wash your hands?"

"Aww, Janey—"

"Go and do it, young man."

"I'm going. I'm going," he said sheepishly. "I just wanted you to see my tree before I washed."

"Well now, I have seen your tree and it is a fine tree. So, go wash your hands and I shall see you at the dinner table."

As her little brother left the room and she began putting away all her of her mother's treasures, Jane suddenly felt a twinge of fear and doubt whisper through her mind. She pushed the dark thoughts away and began to get ready. Nothing would spoil this euphoria that coursed through her veins like a strong drug.

Chapter 8

Dr. Richard Rydell was prompt for dinner. He was literally treated like royalty by Cole. And Hannah was all smiles as she waited on him. Jane actually caught her winking at her and nodding toward the doctor. Jane knew well what she was doing. Like Mr. Porter, Hannah believed Jane was overdue for catching the interest of an eligible young man of stature. Jane smiled a secret smile, thinking instead of Emma and the feel of her lips. They all would be shocked to know who really set her heart aflutter.

Emma sat quiet and regal, looking every bit a queen, beside Henry. She hadn't offered much to the dinner conversation. After Cole and Dr. Rydell exhausted all the topics that men found stimulating—and usually confined to smokey, private men's rooms—Hannah cleared the table of dessert. Emma unexpectedly pulled back from the table and promptly excused herself, pleading illness.

Jane watched her, alarmed, as she dabbed her lips with her napkin. Emma did not look ill, but perhaps it had been all the extra cream and cheese in Hannah's extravagant dessert, cheesecake.

Although Jane tried to catch Emma's eye, Emma would not even look at her. She instead lowered her head and rushed from the table. Concerned and desperate to follow her, Jane knew she would draw suspicion. It would be terribly rude to leave the table without an adequate explanation and chasing after a member of the staff was hardly acceptable. So, she indulged Henry as he rattled on and attempted to make his napkin look like a rabbit as Emma had done. Hannah entered the room with a pot of coffee and walked to her side.

"Coffee, Miss Jane, or would you prefer tea?"

"No, thank you, Hannah," Jane said, "I should put Henry to bed soon anyway." She thought it was as good an excuse as any to get away and see after Emma.

"Awe, Janey, but we only just finished dinner and I want to show Dr. Rydell my painting that Cole did."

"Don't be obstinate, young man," Jane said, growing more impatient each minute that ticked by. She felt a tinge of guilt for chastising Henry.

"The boy is right," Cole said. "He can stay up late. Why not take Henry to his room for the painting so he can bring it down to the doctor." He laughed and turned to Dr. Rydell. "Although I warn you, my good doctor, my little brother here is making too big a fuss about a painting of no real worth."

Jane was certainly pleased to see Cole so full of vigor. Dr. Rydell seemed to have formed a bond with her brother and she welcomed that, but she did not welcome his attentions to Emma. He had spent much of the evening gazing her way. Emma had no interest in him, of course, but it could get difficult if the doctor insisted on calling after Emma and courting her. Jane struggled to put that horrid scenario out of her head.

"Come, Henry, you heard Cole. Let's go and fetch the painting."

She got up and reached out for him. "If you'll excuse us," she said, smiling at Cole and Dr. Rydell. "Henry and I shall return."

Jane grabbed Henry and literally lifted him away from his chair, the white napkin that looked nothing like a rabbit, left crumpled on the seat. They both ran up the main staircase and down the hall to his room. Jane wanted to stop at Emma's room next door, but instead, she helped Henry take the painting down from the wall. She made sure he had a good hold of it and pointed him down the hall.

"You go on back downstairs, Henry. I want to check in on Emma and see if she needs anything. We don't want her being so sick and all alone, do we?"

Henry eyed her with uncertainty. "Cole will be expecting you, you know."

She reached out and took hold of his shoulder. "I know, dear. I shan't be long. I will be down shortly. Please, Henry, go on now."

He hesitated for a few seconds and then hurried away, the painting tucked under his gangly arm. As soon as she saw him round the corner and out of sight, she nearly ran to Emma's door.

"Emma," she whispered, her lips pressed close to the door. She knocked lightly. At first, there was no answer and she feared that perhaps Emma had gone to sleep or worse, that she might be too ill. She knocked again. "Emma, it's Jane. I've come to see if you're in need of anything."

She heard the doorknob turn and Emma stood in the open doorway, her blue robe wrapped around her.

"Jane, I was not expecting to see you tonight." She opened the door to allow her to slip through.

For a fleeting moment, Jane thought she saw a troubled expression cross Emma's face. But then it was gone, replaced with a smile that melted away any doubt. The room was ablaze with candles that cast soft shadows in every corner.

"Has Dr. Rydell gone?" Emma asked.

"No. I left the dinner table with him and Cole still conversing. I had to find an excuse to leave, and poor Henry provided me a perfect one. He wanted to show the doctor the painting that Cole had done of him so I accompanied him to his room."

"And you sent him downstairs alone?"

"Yes, I did. I wanted to see you. Be alone with you."

Emma did not greet her with the anticipation she'd expected. Not even a touch. Instead, she walked slowly to the table beside her bed, where she had several candles burning and a large, leather-bound book. There was a strong, not unpleasant smell in the room. It was not perfume but wisps of smoke floated through the air.

Jane suddenly noticed that the oversized trunk Emma had brought with her sat open on the floor. Inside was a series of shelves, and Jane was fascinated at the assorted bottles and jars sitting along the silk-covered shelving.

"I'm sorry, Emma, I...thought...I didn't think you might be sleeping or ready for bed."

Inside, Jane's heart was feeling like a shattered piece of glass. Emma did not want her. She did not crave her the same way Jane wanted Emma. She did not burn for the touch of her skin. Jane shook the painful thoughts from her head and glanced at the book on the desk.

"What were you reading? If I am disturbing you, I can go away..."

"Nonsense." Emma reached out and grabbed her arm. "I never want you to go away." She closed the book on the desk, carefully tucking a ribbon at the point where she'd left off. "I stopped at the library and picked out a volume of Shakespeare. I was reading *Hamlet*. Have you read it?"

Relief washed over Jane. Emma did want her and was perhaps just in a mood or still feeling sick.

90

"No," she admitted. "It was rather too difficult for me. All those archaic words and expressions were too taxing, I'm afraid. I know from the Colonel that *Hamlet* is a very sad book. And it must be true because you looked so misty-eyed and distant when I walked in." She wanted so much to reach out and touch Emma's cheek, but something held her back.

Emma gazed at her closely. "You're right, Jane. It is a sad story. It's about a man who decides to avenge a great wrong that had been done to him..." She stopped and looked away to one of the flickering candles. "You really should try and read it again sometime. I think you might grow fond of it."

She set her fierce blue eyes upon Jane. "But enough about *Hamlet*. Does something trouble you, Jane?"

Jane giggled nervously, not sure why or what exactly was bothering her. "I suppose I can never hide much from you."

Emma walked to the open trunk and pulled out a large bottle filled with a lovely green liquid. Jane wondered if it was another of her wondrous and potent oils.

"Come, Jane, join me in toasting the green fairy. This will surely loosen your tongue—" She looked at Jane and smiled seductively. "It has been known to unleash the beast within us all."

"Green fairy?" Jane asked as she watched Emma bring out two oddly shaped, small glasses and a petite box covered in purple velvet.

"It's the name given to this drink in certain circles. Sit down on the bed, Jane. I shall make the drinks. Watch me."

Emma put the bottle of the mysterious green liquid, the two funny little glasses and the purple velvet box on the desk. She then grabbed a pitcher of water from the bureau.

91

"I stopped in the kitchen for the pitcher of iced water. I'm afraid the ice has already melted, but it's cold nonetheless. A glass of Absinthe always makes me feel better, no matter what ails me." She walked over to Jane and placed a soft kiss on her lips, leaving Jane only wanting more.

Jane watched as Emma took the cork from the bottle and poured about a half-glass full of the opaque green spirit into each glass. She then opened the purple box and pulled from it a shiny spoon that didn't really look much like a regular spoon. It had curious little star cutouts along the part where the bowl should have been, but it was mostly flat. Jane was entranced with the ritual. This was a totally exhilarating and new thing for her!

"All bohemians consume Absinthe, my sweet Jane. We call it "the green fairy" because of its color." Emma placed the spoon atop one of the glasses.

"Who are bohemians?"

"People who are outsiders, Jane. People like me, who live along the fringes of proper society. People who don't fit inside a perfect little box, like this one." She pulled a smallish cube of sugar out of the small box and set it atop the oddly fashioned spoon. "Now, in order to make the real magic happen with the Absinthe, we add a bit of cold water."

Emma slowly poured water from the pitcher over the sugar cube on the spoon. Jane watched as the cube began to dissolve and the slushy blend dripped down through the cut-out stars, mixing with the green alcohol in the glass.

To Jane's complete surprise, the drink turned a milky, frothy color with only a hint of the original green. Emma watched her intently as she handed Jane the glass.

"The nectar of the gods, my dear Jane. I make the Absinthe myself. The secret, powerful ingredient is the

Artemisia absinthian, more commonly known as wormwood root. One must take care because wormwood root contains thujone, which can be a deadly toxin if one consumes too much..."

She paused as she repeated the ritual with the other glass. "I also add green anise, sweet fennel, angelica root, coriander and sweet fly."

Emma sat, drink in hand, beside Jane on the bed.

"Emma, this isn't going to give me a dreadful headache in the morning, is it?" Jane smiled as she eyed the milky liquid with interest.

"Drink it, Jane. I can guarantee nothing." Emma took the first sip, watching Jane over the rim of the glass.

Jane brought the glass to her lips and tasted a small drop. It was slightly bitter with a strong aftertaste of licorice, but not altogether off putting.

Emma ran her hand down Jane's arm. "Now, tell me, what troubles you so that you left the dinner table and your esteemed guest?"

The candles in the room cast tiny flickers of fire that seemed to dance in the blueness of Emma's piercing gaze. Jane wasn't sure if it was already the effects of the strange drink, but her insides felt as if they were melting.

"I so want to tell Cole about us, Emma. I do. I mean, not about, well, the us beneath the wisteria, but I want him to know that we are close friends. That you are not just Henry's governess, a common household servant..." She studied her lover but Emma said nothing, and took another drink.

"Oh, Emma, he needs to know but he is so stubborn and stuck in the old ways and uppity moral codes and class discrimination."

"Dear Jane, you should be very proud of him. The Havens name is a great name in these parts, and Cole is naturally proud of his status. You don't expect him to give up on that so easily, do you? After all, it isn't everyone who can say that their father rode side by side with Sherman in the war."

Emma took another, bigger sip of the Absinthe and Jane followed suit, not wanting to appear ungrateful or unappreciative.

"You're right, of course. The Colonel was a great man." Jane was beginning to like the aftertaste of the anise and drank more.

"Yes," Emma nodded. "And like all great men, he probably had his foibles. However—" A faint smile flickered on her face. "—that is not necessarily always viewed as an evil."

"Foibles?" Jane asked, her head a bit foggy. "I don't understand."

"Oh, forgive me, dearest. I did not intend to mention it."

"You are always so vague," Jane insisted. "Please be more clear, Emma. What were you intending to say?"

"I simply meant," Emma said gently, "That all great families have a skeleton hidden deep in the closet. Part of tradition, I suppose. A rumor, a bit of gossip." She put her hand on Jane's shoulder. "You should never feel bad about something that is no more than an ill-spoken tale."

Jane suddenly felt the candlelight in the room grow brighter and the shadows loomed larger. "If you're referring to the story that my father and some lady he met during the war—"

"Yes. I meant that." Emma's eyed Jane intently.

"Where did you hear that?"

"In town, when I arrived here. Perhaps the old gossips of Havens Falls hoped to run me out of town by shocking me."

Emma held Jane's hand and kissed her fingers slowly, one by one. "My darling Jane, the Colonel was a lusty, full-blooded man. He was returning from a brutal war. Your mother was gone."

Jane nodded, her head feeling as light as the smoke from the candles.

"I know, I know and I understand, except for the ugly gossip about..." She paused. "...About a child. If there was indeed a child—"

Emma turned away and drank more of the Absinthe, her glass nearly empty. "Jane, I seriously doubt that part of the tale. Your father was only a man, returning home from the war. Doesn't the upper crust of your society normally accept this from their men? Was there a child conceived from the comfort your Colonel sought in the arms of a stranger? No one can prove it. Certainly, it would be beyond cruel to believe."

Emma emptied her glass of the Absinthe and got up to mix another. "Jane, there is plenty of the Absinthe for multiple drinks for the both of us, you know, but you aren't keeping up." She cast a coy smile at her.

"I didn't want to get so tipsy that I make no sense." Jane laughed, as she took one deep swallow. "You're right, Emma, it would be too cruel and my father was not a cruel man. No one has ever produced evidence to support those horrid tales. It would be too difficult to imagine a poor child, fatherless all these years, never knowing who his or her father was, or that they even had a family." She took more of the drink.

Emma came back and sat even closer to Jane on the bed. She stared intently at her and suddenly began to remove the pins from Jane's perfectly coifed hair. As the auburn waves fell down Jane's back and shoulders, Emma ran her fingers through her luxurious hair.

"You are so beautiful, it is almost painful," Emma whispered softly into Jane's ear.

Jane closed her eyes and thought she felt the room shift and move under her feet. The heat from the candles caressed her skin. When she opened her eyes, everything in the room wavered and flickered in rhythm with the candle flames, even Emma. She seemed to bend and shimmer.

Jane drank the last of the bitter brew, her heart beat suddenly thudding in her ears. She was so hot that she wanted desperately to remove every single piece of clothing to let the heat racing through her body escape.

Emma emptied her glass of Absinthe in one swallow, her gaze wild and hot on Jane. She then stood up and stripped her robe off, flinging it on the bed. Tonight, she had no nightshirt beneath, only her naked body.

"Look at me, Jane. Shall we make love with wild abandon while the others are all downstairs and no one can hear us?"

Jane could not remove her eyes from the pale, smooth and tempting body of Emma Stiles. The desire between her thighs swelled to a feverish passion.

"Oh, Lord forgive me, but I need you more than the breath I inhale," she whispered.

"You need air to breathe, food to eat and water to drink. I don't want you to merely need me, Jane. I want you to want me."

Jane arose and approached Emma and stood so close, she could smell the sweet aroma of the Absinthe on her breath, her lips wet with the liquor.

"I want you more than anything I have ever wanted in my life." She kissed the full, plump lips, the hunger growing. Jane began to remove her dress as Emma helped her at a hurried pace, their desires ready to be fulfilled.

When Jane's last undergarment lay in a crumpled pile beneath her feet, she cast her eyes once again at the bare and lovely Emma. It was only then, in the room that shimmered in dancing candlelight, that Jane saw the white, narrow scars that streaked Emma's shoulders, arms and stomach. In the darkness of the night under the wisteria, she had not seen them.

Emma met her gaze and quietly explained. "I learned to punish myself for all those sins I collected, my darling." She looked away. "When the horror of what I had to do, when I became so gorged with other's sins, I just had to scrub the filth off my body. But soap and water and a sponge wasn't enough."

Deep pain and sorrow gripped Jane's heart. "My darling Emma—"

"Show me no pity," Emma said in a strong voice. "I couldn't wash myself clean like others could with a bath. No, I took off to the woods. I broke branches off trees and rode their hard bark and leaves, as hard as I could, over my body until my skin was raw, broke and bleeding."

She reached out and embraced Jane tightly.

"I've stripped myself down completely for you, Jane, body and soul. Now, do you want me, still?"

"If I could peel my flesh open to you, I could show you how much I love you, and how my heart beats and aches for you," Jane whispered in a voice that sounded far away and out of breath. Was the liquor affecting her senses?

She began to kiss the pale, delicate scars that snaked down Emma's shoulders and then worked her mouth further down the length of one arm, licking each scar lightly, delicately. Emma's skin tasted of the strong oil they had used the first night of love-making. Jane brought her mouth to Emma's perfectly formed breasts, her erect nipples hard enough to bite. And she did, just enough to elicit a soft moan from Emma, who closed her eyes and leaned her head.

"Jane," she said in a raspy whisper, "Cole, Henry, the doctor, they will wonder—"

"Shhh," Jane said, kneeling down before Emma. "There is only you and me."

She took hold of Emma's hips and kissed the dark mass of hair between her legs. "I want every single piece of you, Emma." She got up and embraced Emma tightly, hungrily kissing her, tongue deep inside her mouth. "We shall belong to each other, always."

Emma pulled her away and led her to the bed. "Stay with me tonight, my dear Jane. We shall make love until the morning sun."

Jane held on fiercely to Emma. She almost feared letting go, for the room was twisting and transforming into unrecognizable shapes. Only Emma remained real. It had to be the Absinthe. But her fears of the hallucinations flooding her brain were nothing compared to the fierce passions blazing inside her.

As they both fell into the bed, Jane faintly heard the distinct click of boots outside in the hall. But everything in her head seemed surreal, unreal, belonging to another world not her own.

"Cole," she whispered.

Emma kissed her, pressing her down with her body.

"He doesn't belong in our world in here, Jane. Make love to me, now."

Jane knew that she was committing an unforgivable and scandalous sin. But she had abandoned everything she had held sacred in exchange for loving another woman. No, she would not leave Emma's bed tonight.

As they made the most passionate love, Jane saw the wild flames that danced eerily from the candles in the room. They rose and fell with the rhythm of their bodies.

***

The next morning, on her way down to breakfast, Jane met Hannah Browne at the foot of the landing. The housekeeper's round face wore a solemn, almost alarmed look. Puzzled and somewhat disturbed, Jane kept a slight smile.

"Am I the first one up?" Jane had found her way to her room before sunrise, head and thoughts muddled and foggy. Making love in Emma's arms all night, and overindulgence in Absinthe, had taken a toll. The green fairy was surely the Devil's brew. She was not sure she would drink it again, even at Emma's urging.

"Never you mind who is up first," Hannah said brusquely. "Cole is up and waiting for you in the study." Her eyes avoided Jane's.

"Hannah, what has gotten into you? Are you now insulting me by not even speaking to my face?"

The older woman glared back at Jane. "It isn't me that's changed, Miss Jane." She shook her head. "No, not me. I only know what I see—" She stopped and put a hand on her chest. "I know what I see in my heart."

Jane's stomach tightened. Did Hannah know about Emma and her? She couldn't possibly know. She was just being her rude self.

"Well, go on, Miss Jane. Cole is in a mood this morning. Don't know what happened between last night and this morning." She shook her head one last time and left Jane fearful of meeting her brother for the first time in her life.

As Jane worked her way slowly to the study, she knew Cole would be livid with her behavior last night. He had every right to be. To leave an invited guest waiting and never return was not what a proper lady did. It was irresponsible. Two things Jane had always prided herself in were her dependability and her responsibility. Good, dependable Jane. Boring Jane. She would not ask for forgiveness. She would apologize because she had been wrong. But Jane felt alive for the first time since the Colonel passed away and she would never go back to being good, dependable, boring and unhappy Jane.

She knocked and opened the study doors. Cole stood, glass filled with his preferred liquor of the day. The fact that he was drinking anything at all this early in the morning was already a bad omen.

"Well, Jane rises early this morning." He raised the glass to her, his face without mirth. "How unlike you, sister."

"And how like you to find a drink in your hand this early." It hurt her after she'd said it. The last thing she wanted was to bring grief and pain to her family.

She moved towards him. "Oh Cole, I had thought that with you painting again, you might leave—" She pointed to the glass in his hand. "I hoped you'd quit drinking."

"I didn't call to see you to discuss my habits, dear Jane, but yours. Or more specifically, your bad ones." He swallowed what was left in the glass.

Jane expected Cole to be disappointed and upset over her behavior last night, but it hurt her to think one incident could send him back to the bottle.

"Cole, I acted improperly and irresponsibly last night and owe you and Dr. Rydell apologies," she said in a soft voice, her eyes downcast.

"I should say so. Indeed. Forget me, but to leave the dinner table where an esteemed and invited guest was still seated and never return is very distasteful and unladylike." He turned and headed for the bottle.

"Cole, no, not so early, please." Jane followed him.

He ignored her as he poured another full glass. "Your concern for Miss Stiles is unhealthy and questionable. I stopped by your room last night after bidding the doctor good night. He was very concerned about Miss Stiles and feared her quite ill after you did not return. He offered to go up and see if he could help. I persuaded him not to worry, that you would send word of her condition if it warranted a doctor's services. We are already in debt to him for saving Henry." His eyes were cold as he stared at Jane.

"You were not in your room last night, Jane. I knocked twice and since your door was open, I entered. Your bed was still made."

So it was Cole she had heard walking the hall last night. Jane saw his knuckles grow white in anger and a darkness overcome his face. "Did you stay the night in Miss Stiles' room?"

Jane swallowed hard. She felt like a heavy stone had been dropped against her chest.

"Her stomach was very sick, Cole. It must have been the cheesecake. I decided I should stay until she felt better and fell asleep on the chair. It was the least kindness I could afford her." Jane thought her voice sounded small and weak. She had never lied before.

Cole walked to the wingback chair and took a big swig of the liquor. "It's quite obvious that when it comes to Miss Stiles, our conversation regarding staff and our relationship with said staff fell on deaf ears."

Jane gathered up her courage. It was now or never. "She is my friend, Cole." She found her voice and blurted out what she'd been so afraid to say to her brother. "I will not be ashamed to claim her as a dear friend and will not see her or treat her as another staff member. I do for her the same as I do for you or Henry or any other person I hold dear."

She almost winced, waiting for the fury that would surely come. Instead and to her complete surprise, Cole's shoulders suddenly slumped and a loud sigh escaped his lips. He looked at her with helplessness in his eyes.

"So, I am now a more miserable failure than I was before. I've not only failed Henry, but I've been unable to find you a husband or tame your rebellious heart."

"Cole, I am not a stable horse that needed to be tamed. I am a woman who for once knows who she is and what she wants. Please don't blame my friendship with Miss Stiles for your own feelings of inadequacy. Please assure me this is not what has led you back to the bottle. It cannot be. Friendship and even love should never be dependent or divided by class or status in life. The affairs of the heart are pure and free of the confines of our society."

Cole sighed even as he attempted a smile. "Life is not the fantasy you live in, my dear sister. We must interact and live within the rules or be cast out as an outsider."

Outsider. Bohemian. Emma's words rushed into Jane's heart. They were words of pain. Her thoughts filled with the memory of the pain and scars her beloved Emma wore because she had been cast out by society.

"If that's the society I must be forced to live in, then I would rather embrace the curse of being thought an outsider." Jane nearly whispered the words.

Cole sat down in the chair, a distant look in his eyes.

"So what shall you do when your Miss Stiles leaves us, Jane? She will be gone. Once her work with Henry is done, I will have no further need of her. You will be lonely again and I shall have my bottle." He cast a crooked smile at her. "But we'll always have each other."

Jane shook her head. "I will not go back to the miserable, suffocating life I had before Emma came." She stopped, realizing she had used Emma's given name.

"Emma," Cole repeated. "So it is Emma that has brought all the magic to this house, then?"

"Yes," Jane said enthusiastically. "Yes, Cole. Can't you see all the positive changes she has brought to Henry, to me, to..." she paused, "...to you."

Cole ran a hand through his unruly hair, leaning his head back on the chair.

"Go away, Jane. The only thing I feel now is a headache. I shall make sure I offer your apology to Dr. Rydell when I see him next, assuming he will even accept another dinner invitation from us."

"Cole...I'm sorry about last night."

No, I'm not sorry about you, Emma. Jane pushed back the thoughts of passion, of Emma's shimmering body and yes, beautiful scars.

"God help us all, Jane," Cole said, a defeated tone to his voice.

"God helps those who help themselves." She went to her brother and knelt down beside him, taking his hand. "Cole, Havenswood, Henry and I need you to be the man that is in here..." She placed her hand upon his chest. "Please, forgive me for disappointing you. But please, keep painting that splendid scene I saw in the art room. It is within you to create beauty."

He gazed at her with empty eyes and a sad frown. "I have nothing left, I'm afraid. If I died today, no one would give a damn."

Jane shot back up. "You stop speaking like that. My brother, the son of Colonel Vincent Havens, does not speak thus."

He waved her away. "Go, Jane. My headache grows worse."

Though she loved her brother with all her heart, Jane had had all she could handle of his drinking and his moodiness. As she turned away and walked out of the room, she heard the smashing of glass as she closed the doors behind her.

Chapter 9

"*H*ow long has he been like this, Miss Havens?"

"We've been unable to rouse him since I returned home late afternoon. I am so thankful that I had invited you to dinner—"

Jane had thought to mend fences with Dr. Rydell and a dinner invitation might be a perfect excuse to apologize personally.

"Never mind that now. He's apparently taken an overdose of sleeping draught. We must wake him before it's too late."

Jane was riddled with guilt for disappointing her brother and arguing with him the night before. If he died, it was surely her fault!

"He looks so terrible. So waxy and lifeless."

"Yes," Dr. Rydell said briskly, his tone sounding urgent. "It's a tell-tale sign of drugs."

Cole suddenly opened his eyes and Jane saw that he tried to speak, but no words came from his mouth.

"Doctor!"

Emma, who stood next to Jane, came forward. "Shall I get some water?"

"Yes, we'll need plenty of it," the doctor said.

Emma left, nearly running out of the room and came back quickly with a bucket of water.

"Here, place some in the wash bin right there on the night stand—we shall need to hurry before it is too late for Cole. Where is Mrs. Browne with the mustard and iodine? He is need of an emetic—and fast."

Jane bent over Cole and tenderly brushed his cheeks and stray hair from his face.

"Please come back to us, Cole, please." She took his hand and squeezed it.

Hannah burst through the door, her hands full of brown bottles and a bowl with several eggs.

"Quick, mix this amount of each with the water in the wash bin," Dr. Rydell said, handing Hannah a piece of paper with measurements. He pointed to the night stand.

The mixture was foul-smelling and Jane did everything to cover her nose. Could that wild concoction really save her brother? She had sent Emma to sit with Henry. The last thing they needed was him adding to the confusion in the room.

Dr. Rydell took out a long piece of narrow green tubing from his black bag and attached a small funnel to one end. Jane watched in shocked silence as the doctor forced the other end of the tube down deep into Cole's throat, causing him to gag.

"Quickly, Mrs. Browne! Bring the wash basin here. Pour it all into the funnel now!"

A flush of the watery, smelly mix washed down the tube into Cole's throat. He immediately began shaking as he swallowed and his stomach bloated with the vile liquid.

Suddenly, he sat up and started to vomit uncontrollably. The stink of the mustard, iodine and eggs was overpowering. Cole finally lay back, wiping his mouth and gasping for air. The potent emetic had hopefully cleaned out most of the drug in his stomach.

Jane saw her brother hold his stomach and moan in relief. Her gaze fell on the foul-looking mess on the floor.

105

She could no longer fight the sick churning in her own stomach. She ran out of the room in a hurry, hoping she could reach the sink in time.

***

The next morning, Old Gabe helped Cole to the cool shadows of the portico. He stayed there all day to bring some fresh air into his lungs. Hannah fixed the hammock, with its polka dotted covers, into an excellent substitute for a bed. Propped up against large, fluffy pillows, Cole enjoyed the warm June breezes that promised a hot summer. He remained, however, as fussy and morose as ever, even after Hannah plied him with hot broths and tall, cool glasses of fruit juices.

Both Jane and Henry took turns keeping him company. Cole remained unkempt, his hair spilling down into his eyes, his pale face unshaven. He only stared glassily at the sky.

The day was filled with chirping birds, the thickets alive with cicadas and crickets. Jane didn't know what to make of her brother's catatonic behavior. She was feeling more and more responsible for causing the whole horrid episode. The guilt simmered constantly in her heart.

She came out to the porch and sat on one of the wicker chairs. She took one of his hands and squeezed hard.

"Cole, you must talk to me."

He stared blankly at her and shook his head slowly.

"We must speak, please. It's important I know what caused this terrible state. I cannot bear it, Cole, if I were to be the cause of your pain. Do you understand?"

He tried to turn away, but she gently turned his stubby face until their eyes met. His eyes suddenly watered and he sagged against her chest.

"Oh, Jane. I am a shameful man."

"Nonsense."

He pushed away from her. "I cannot even keep control of my household. Any man would be ashamed. Why should I react differently?"

"Because you are a Havens."

"And that is precisely why I wanted to drink myself into oblivion. I was certain the sleep potion chaser would guarantee a swift end to my pain."

Jane was surprised and saddened by her brother's loss of spirit. His willingness to die sickened her.

"Cole, how could you mix alcohol and laudanum? And how did you get the laudanum? I'm certain Hannah didn't give it to you, and I don't believe Emma, if she had some, would leave it in view considering the inebriated state you were in."

He turned his face away. "What does it matter where it came from? I had some of it. I wanted everything and everyone to go away. Even now—"

"Hush," Jane said sternly. "Do not talk like that. Cole, have you considered that maybe you try too hard? Maybe you shouldn't take it upon yourself to try and control people. Help yourself and nurture Havenswood, instead of molding it and us into whatever you think society expects of us."

She reached out and touched his shoulder.

"Please, Cole, stop drinking. Do it for me. For Henry. For God's sake, just don't use me as an excuse to get drunk. I cannot live day in and day out seeing you destroy yourself."

He gazed intensely at her. "Can you promise me that you will drop your impetuous friendship with the governess and never try that insanity again?"

Jane rose angrily to her feet.

"Insanity? Impetuous? It was not I that took an overdose of sleep draught, Cole. You did." Believing she had spoken too harshly, Jane cast her gaze to the floor. "I have done nothing wrong or insane by befriending Emma Stiles."

Her brother did not answer, and that frustrated Jane further. She turned away and saw the carriage coming around the corner of Havenswood, leading away from the barn. Gabe and Hannah Browne sat, all attired in their Sunday best, on the buckboard of their rig. Gabe wore his dark suit and cravat, and Hannah sat primly beside him, with her brightly colored sunbonnet tied beneath her chin. They both looked joyous.

Gabe wheeled the rig alongside the portico and halted the two old, elegant English Draft horses.

"Just wanted to stop by on the way to church to inquire after your health, Master Cole."

"Can't complain, I suppose," Cole said, unconvincingly. "Thank you for your concern."

"You look very nice, Hannah," Jane added.

Hannah nodded, clasping her sprig of roses. "We'll be praying for Master Cole."

"Expecting to be back at noontime, Master Cole, Miss Jane," Gabe said as he swung the rig out toward the roadway, the two large horses leading evenly, if not a bit hesitantly. Not too far behind, on the road, Henry and Goldy sauntered toward then.

"Well now," Cole murmured, eyes focused on the door to the house, "Here comes your Miss Stiles. I shall leave you two in private until dinner." He nodded toward the double doors to the portico.

Jane's gaze went to Emma. "As you wish, Cole."

Emma was walking toward them, her slender figure seemed to glide in her full flowing skirt. She was as composed as always, unlike the vixen she turned into when they made love. Composed was not a word Jane would equate with the fire Emma wielded in the throes of passion.

She nodded at Cole and smiled at Jane, but then they both saw the birth of terror in her blue eyes. Her hands flew up to her face and her gaze fixed on the roadway leading from the house.

The rig bearing Gabe and Hannah had suddenly began to veer from left to right, lurching, and then moving erratically. Gabe appeared to be having trouble handling the horses. They had risen in sudden protest, pawing the air with their hooves. Gabe's bellowing voice attempted to still them.

Cole, Jane and Emma watched as Gabe stood up on the buckboard, flashing the whip. It wasn't working. Suddenly, with a swift, forward burst of speed, the horses shot ahead, bolting faster than Jane had ever seen them run before. Gabe Browne was flung backwards onto the seat, stumbling and trying to regain the reins.

The rig jounced and jarred as Hannah screamed. The old man shouted at the horses again, but it was obvious something was very wrong. The wild horses surged ahead, tearing toward the gateway at astounding speed. And running into their path were Henry and Goldy!

Cole uttered an oath and ran off the portico, his coat tails flying. Emma took off after him, keeping up with the still weakened Cole. Jane followed the both of them, trailing behind.

Cole could not catch up with Gabe and the out-of-control wagon. Thankfully, Emma snatched Henry just short of careening into their path.

Protecting her owner, Goldy barked ferociously, and nipped at the horses' hooves. Everyone watched in horror as their beloved Golden Retriever ran in front of the stomping feet. He would be trampled.

"Goldy, come back boy!" Henry cried out.

Emma suddenly ran furiously toward Goldy and flung herself at the dog, shoving him out of the way. The horses and cart careened past them in a flurry of choking dust clouds.

Cole ran to Emma, who was nearly face down in the grass, holding on to the squirming and frightened Goldy.

"Are you all right, Miss Stiles?" He was gasping, trying to catch his breath.

That's when Henry rushed across the road and came to hug his dog tightly.

He cried softly until Goldy began to lick his face, unhurt.

"I'm fine, Mr. Havens." Emma stood up and dusted the fine dirt and grass from her skirt and blouse.

Jane reached them, holding back the urge to rush in and hold Emma too tight. She had saved Goldy, putting her own life in jeopardy. The three of them watched as the rig continued racing wildly ahead and then suddenly veered sideways into a ditch, with a grinding sound of crying horses, spinning wheels and screaming voices.

They all ran toward the ditched cart as fast as they could. Hannah Browne had been thrown from the rig and lay struggling on the grass. Gabe was shoved against the side of the buckboard, grimacing in pain and trying to reach his wife.

"Hannah! Hannah!"

Cole jumped up on the leaning rig, prodding the old man's body for broken bones. Jane's vision began to swim. Her heart was beating faster than the poor run-away mares. Another calamity had befallen Havenswood. What was happening?

"Jane!" She heard Emma call out her name in fear.

But Jane heard no more. The world around her was growing darker. Havenswood was falling, falling, falling.

The columns and the portico were toppling, toppling, the arched doorways crumbling, and the slanted rooftop sliding into a dark sea of roiling cauldron of doom.

"Emma..." It was all she could mutter. The sun suddenly went black. She could take no more.

Chapter 10

*B*y one of God's miracles, the Browne's had not been killed or even seriously injured. Certainly, there were injuries, but nothing that would not mend and heal. Hannah had narrowly avoided getting crushed beneath the tipped rig. She had a bruised shoulder and a large gash on her right arm. Gabe only suffered a bruised right arm.

Cole had to destroy the beautiful English Drafts, using the Colonel's old 52-caliber Sharps rifle, which had ironically hung unused in the master bedroom all these years since their father's death. Fortunately for Jane, she didn't have to watch the slaughter of the injured horses; she had mercifully fainted.

Dr. Rydell, summoned by Cole, had ridden out to Havenswood almost immediately. If any of them had ever doubted his ability as a physician, their misgivings were thoroughly dispelled by his masterful mending of the beaten and bruised Brownes.

Young Henry had been ordered to his room and allowed to keep Goldy. Emma offered to keep them company. Jane was sure Emma could manage all the questions Henry's inquisitive mind could muster. What she desperately wanted most was to fall into the comforting arms of her lover, but it seemed that the dark cloud over Havenswood was conspiring to keep them apart.

Jane walked Dr. Rydell to the living room where they found Cole moodily staring into the fireplace. Jane was saddened to notice the bottle of brandy in plain view on the table near his chair. Yet somehow, this time, she could almost understand his need for drowning in the brandy. In times of distress, everyone found a way to cope with tragedy. The difference was that Cole sought solace in a bottle while she craved the body of Emma Stiles.

Both Jane and Cole were fond of the Brownes and Cole had to shoot two horses. They had been their last link to their father, the Colonel, who had imported them from England more than a decade before. Cole had helped his father train the prized horses, and Jane knew he was heart-sick for putting them down.

Dr. Rydell was sympathetic. His even toned voice and casual quality of his remarks were always welcomed.

"Mr. and Mrs. Browne will both be fine," he said. "They are a stout couple. I've administered some morphine to relieve some of the pain, but with rest and quiet, they should be back around in a couple of weeks, maybe, or less."

"Yes," Cole said bitterly, "and who knows, we may all be dead if we continue to live in Havenswood. How ironic."

Dr. Rydell looked at Jane and then back at Cole.

"How so?"

"Well, my good doctor, we should offer you room and board here at Havenswood. So far, four of my household have been your patients in a little more than a week. Wouldn't you consider that strange?"

"Perhaps, although I should be more disposed to call it a streak of bad luck. These things do happen that way sometimes."

Cole shook his head and reached for his glass. "Call it what you like. You may help yourself to the bottle, if you like. I have." He shook his head again. "I have never known our family fortunes to be so unlucky."

"It will pass, Cole," Jane interjected, looking at both Cole and the doctor. "Soon, the luck will come back to us."

"Will it? I doubt that," her brother said with a smirk. He poured the brandy into the snifter and paused the glass just before his lips. "The Devil may catch us before then."

Dr. Rydell sat down on the chair at his side and smiled tolerantly. "Look, Cole, I don't wonder that you feel angry and suspicious. I agree that all these accidents would tend to make you think that your family has been singled out for misfortune. As a doctor, all I can offer is that all of this could have been a great deal worse."

"Yes, I know," Cole said, waving the thought away. "Henry could have drowned, I could have died, and the Browne's could have broken their necks. Odd..." He paused and stared at Rydell directly. "Do you know why those two well-trained, docile mares bolted?"

Neither suggested an answer. Cole ran a hand through his thick locks and looked at both the doctor and Jane.

"I have a theory," Cole announced. "I checked all their rigging and what I found puzzled and concerned me. Both of the horses had grossly mounted bridles. They must have been in great discomfort. Poor Gabe had no idea. I know how much he loved those horses and I implicitly trust him with any horse in our stable. He has cared for our animals for decades. He can rig a horse in his sleep." His gaze settled on Jane. "It is not possible that Gabe rigged those two horses in such a manner."

"How could that be, Cole?" Jane blurted out.

"Damn me, I don't understand it. Yet." Cole said. "It's all so ridiculous. Who would have wanted to cause such a

114

terrible thing? Who would intentionally hurt the mares or the Brownes? They don't have an enemy in the world."

Dr. Rydell poked his square chin with a thumb. "How about you, Cole? Do *you* have enemies?"

Cole frowned at him. "Surely, I cannot suggest that I am the most liked or respected man in Havens Falls, but it would be hard to believe that any enemy of mine would stoop to something like this. The Brownes are not Havens. It's too unthinkable."

"I agree. Therefore, may I suggest you abandon trying to place blame and see the accident for what it really was. An accident. A regrettable accident, indeed, but an accident all the same."

Cole laughed, turning to Jane. "Most cheerful, isn't he? I suppose as a physician you are almost bound to such optimism. Very well, Richard. I will do what you suggest. But good Lord, I hope this is the last of the bad luck. We Havens have had enough, eh, Jane?"

"Yes," she said softly. "I would say we have."

Cole refilled his glass. Dr. Rydell glanced at the watch that was neatly tucked in his vest pocket.

"I shall call tomorrow and check on the Brownes. They'll be rather sore and in much pain for a few days until it wears off. But they will mend fine. I promise you that. Is Miss Stiles about?"

"She's upstairs," Cole said dully. "With Henry."

"Too bad. I wanted to see her before I left. Just wanted to make sure she was okay after that tumble she took. I still can't seem to get her face out of my mind. I'm certain I've seen her before."

"You rather fancy our Miss Stiles?" Cole asked with a smile and a glance at Jane.

Rydell shrugged, but Jane could see the contradiction in his eyes.

"Do I? Perhaps. If I do, must I ask you first for approval?"

Please, God, no. You will not put your hands on Emma's body. Say no, Cole! Jane's stomach turned and she felt squeamish. She would do whatever was in her power to prevent Dr. Rydell from pursuing Emma.

The two men's eyes locked for a moment, and Jane held her breath. Then her brother relaxed, laughed and held up his glass.

"Do as you like, Richard. I am not her keeper. Miss Stiles is a lovely woman, I admit, though not my type." His attention shifted to Jane. "She seems so remote most of the time, like an untouchable work of art."

Dr. Rydell laughed and Jane wanted to slap the both of them hard. She wanted to bolt out of the room to find the woman they had associated with a painting. How could she stay and listen to them discuss her lover?

"There are men who do not care for the Mona Lisa either," Rydell said, "but there is no accounting for personal taste, is there? Well, I shall be off. Good day to you both."

"I'll see you to the door, Dr. Rydell," Jane offered. She wanted him out of Havenswood. If it were up to her, the Havens would switch doctors. Sure, she was thankful for him saving Henry, and for being there for Cole and the Brownes, but he was interested in Emma and Jane could not abide that.

They left Cole to his brandy bottle and the solitude of his own progressively incoherent musings.

The doctor put on his stiff felt bowler hat, but before he went out the door, he paused for one last word for Jane.

"Miss Havens, keep an eye on your brother. Don't let him sink too far into his depression. I take it he has been imbibing all day. That bodes ill for a man. He can lose his perspective."

"Cole will be all right," Jane answered coolly.

"I'm sure he will. No offense intended." He tipped his hat. "Will you say hello to Miss Stiles for me?"

Jane stiffened. She fought to keep her composure.

"Of course, Doctor." She forced a smile.

"Thank you and good evening, Miss Havens."

"Good night, Dr. Rydell."

Long after his small carriage had disappeared up the road, its night lights all but gone from sight, Jane remained with her back pressed to the front door. Why was everything going so badly? She knew the relationship between Emma and she was going to be difficult, for more than one reason, but added to that were all the inexplicable accidents. Cole was right. It was all rather strange.

Confused, she raced up the stairs to Emma's room, hoping she was there and not with Henry. Jane wanted nothing more than to wrap her arms around her in a tight embrace and cover her with kisses. And not tell her Dr. Rydell asked after her.

***

Jane was relieved to find Henry alone in his room assembling a wooden ship as Goldy slept soundly beside his bed. That meant Emma must be in her room.

Jane knocked on her door and received only a verbal invitation to enter. Emma sat at her desk with her head resting on her hands. She barely paid attention as Jane closed the door behind her and locked it.

"Emma, dearest, what is wrong? Are you hurt?" She rushed over to her. "I've been so worried about you. Were you injured when you rescued Goldy?" Jane gently placed her hand on Emma's shoulder. "Is there anything I can do for you?"

Emma shook her head, looked up into Jane's eyes and smiled weakly.

"I am not harmed, dearest. Forgive me, I am still shaken by what happened." Her gaze shifted away. "I never imagined..." she paused and took Jane's hand. "I am only glad I was able to get to poor Goldy. How is he? Both he and Henry seemed fine when I left them."

"Both of them are fine. I wanted so badly to come to you. I needed to make sure you were not hurt."

Emma had changed out of her soiled dress and looked beautiful in a striped shirt waist and cranberry skirt. Her black hair was braided in one long plait down her back.

Jane bent down and placed a light kiss on Emma's lips. "You saved Goldy, Emma, and by jumping in front of those frightened run-way horses, you may have also saved the Brownes as well."

Emma shook her head, a faraway look in her eyes. "I did nothing special. I was there and I did only what I thought I should."

Jane couldn't help but see the darkness that crept over Emma's mood.

"We're all fine now, darling. I think the best thing to do is to put all this behind us. I shall look after the Browne's until they heal and are back on their feet. It won't be terribly bad handling the dinner chores."

"There are some things that can never be forgotten," Emma said, a distant sound to her voice.

Perhaps Emma preferred time alone. Jane couldn't help feeling a bit slighted, in a way. She'd come out of concern and out of a need to be with her. Hold her. The urge to gather Emma in her arms was nearly overpowering but so far, Emma seemed inclined to dismiss those offerings from her. Jane's heart was deeply wounded. What had happened? What had she done or said to distance Emma from her affections?

Emma finally looked up at her and caressed Jane's hand. "I am so tired, dear Jane. That is all. Perhaps what I need most now is rest."

Jane understood perfectly that she had just been dismissed. Had Emma read her thoughts? She parted with a kiss and a promise to check in on her before turning in for the night.

Confused and hurt, Jane went to her bedroom to ponder what had happened. She sat in the dark without lighting a candle. The atmosphere and her mood became oppressive. For now, there were no answers to her questions, no quenching of her thirst for Emma's attention, and that cut her to the core.

***

Hannah Browne had answers of her own.

Bruised and aching, there was no shadow of doubt in the housekeeper's mind. Jane had never seen her so vehemently positive about anything. It was all perfectly clear in the mind of Hannah. She was convinced she knew what evil had befallen Havenswood and the evil had a name.

"Emma Stiles!" Hannah spat out the name when Jane brought her a cup of tea the next morning. "That witch. It's all her doing."

"Hannah, stop that talk. I won't listen and I forbid you to accuse Emma when you have no proof or reason. You cannot blame her for what has happened."

"Can't I now? Look, Miss Jane, you count on your fingers all that has gone wrong in Havenswood since that woman arrived. Go ahead. Do as I say."

Jane shook her head firmly. "No, I won't. What I will do is count the good things. She's made Henry into a proper little gentleman. She's got Cole painting again and she made me aware of..." She paused, aware she had to be cautious with her comments. Her memories of the passion between her and Emma always caused a flush on her cheeks. "...Emma has made me proud to be a woman."

Hannah snorted, barely able to move the bruised shoulder without grimacing in pain.

"Do tell. And what of the other accidents—is she or is she not responsible for them? Who gave Cole that sleep draught? You know twasn't me or Gabe. I've seen what's in that trunk of hers while cleaning her room. She carries her witch's brews in that thing."

"Hannah, stop it!" Jane's scream was more passionate than she intended. She resented Hannah going through Emma's belongings and accusing her of things that were not true. They couldn't be true. "You don't know what you're saying. You're feverish."

"Am I now?" Hannah smirked, holding up her left hand. "Well, let me count for you. One, Henry nearly drowns. If that good Dr. Rydell hadn't come by, he would have. Two, somehow, Cole had a bottle of laudanum to help him overdose while in a drunken state. Then, those poor horses nearly killed us. Cole told us that the bridles had been ill-adjusted and ill fitted. Tampered with is more like it."

She paused and eyed Jane carefully. "You know as well as I do that Gabe can rig up a horse with his eyes closed. Someone did it on purpose."

"What you're suggesting is too terrible," Jane said, her voice unsteady. No, Emma was not capable of doing those horrid things. She was not capable of such acts. It made no sense. "What purpose would she claim?" Jane asked. "What reason is cause for such awful and evil things?"

"I don't know," Hannah replied grimly. "I only know what the good Lord wants of us. I don't know what the devil wants."

Jane felt a stab of fear clutch her heart and her patience snapped. She'd had enough of Hannah and her hatred of Emma.

"Hannah Browne, I forbid you to talk like this any further. I will not have it!"

"Forbid, is it?" The housekeeper cried, her face crumpling. "You'd better do something, then. Gabe and me, we're old. Next time, she'll kill us."

"I'm going to leave you now, Hannah," Jane said sternly. "Calm down and stop thinking such morbid thoughts. Get some rest, please."

Jane left the housekeeper, troubled and uneasy. What terrible things to say about Emma. And even more troubling, Hannah fully believed them to be true!

More than a little disturbed, Jane sought out Emma. She hadn't gotten a chance to check in on her the evening before and Emma had not come looking for her.

She found her on the veranda. The blue ridged mountains in the distance were brilliantly outlined in the morning sunlight.

"Emma, can we talk?"

"Of course." She smiled. "Henry is doing a written examination I gave him, but that will probably take about twenty minutes or so if he keeps true to other similar exams. It's about the War of Eighteen Twelve and I suspect I shall have to go back and help him understand what I've already taught him. History is not his favorite subject."

Her beauty took Jane's breath away. She looked more a goddess than flesh and blood. Emma wore an off white tea dress of the most intricate lace design. Her raven hair was piled high on her head. Jane found it hard to look at her without wanting to touch her. To ravage her with kisses.

"Emma—" Jane paused. Suddenly, she found herself at a loss for words. What was it exactly that she wanted to say? What could she say?

"Well," Emma smiled even wider, her fierce blue eyes intent on Jane. "Is what you want to tell me a secret?" She leaned in closer to Jane. "Should we whisper?"

"Don't joke, please."

"I'm sorry. I didn't mean to offend you, Jane."

Jane sighed. This was foolish and worse, crazy. She smiled to hide her gloomy demeanor.

"Forgive me, sweetheart," Jane said. "It was I who was rude. It was nothing, really." She had to change the subject before she blurted something stupid. "How are Henry's lessons coming?"

"He's doing splendid. He's a good student. He has a thirst for knowledge, a searching mind. That is always a good quality in a young man his age. As a matter of fact, now that you ask, he has been doing so well that I intend to reward him. We're going on a picnic hike tomorrow to Greenroad Woods."

"Oh, Henry will like that. He's wanted to go on a long hike for some time. I'd love to go with you but I've agreed to see to the Brownes and take care of the dinners. They really need looking after for a bit longer."

Emma and Jane stood so close that Jane could pull her in and kiss her. But she couldn't do that. Not out here. Not in plain view.

"I wish you could join us, my dear Jane. And I want to assure you about Henry's safety. Please don't worry. I shall see that he is safe. We shall be very careful. Never fear. We are even bringing Goldy along."

Jane needed to back away. To fight the temptation that gripped her. Why did Emma Stiles move her in such uncontrollable ways? She could smell the exotic scent of a perfume she did not recognize.

"I know you will be careful, Emma."

Emma reached out and ran her hand over Jane's cheek. "But you are pale, dearest. You really could use a little sun. Are you certain you cannot leave the Brownes for merely a morning?"

Jane leaned her face onto Emma's soft hand and sighed. "Especially not in the morning. I wish I could go with you and Henry. Let's plan for another picnic soon. And you are beginning to sound like Dr. Rydell. He is a great believer in the healing powers of the sunshine."

She smiled and studied the face of the woman that had stolen her heart. A darkness clouded Emma's eyes and she pulled away.

"Really?" Emma said. "Well, he should know. He's the doctor."

Jane peered even closer into Emma's eyes. Now was the perfect time to bring up the fear that had been gnawing at her insides.

"You know, he wants to court you. He's asked Cole if that would be permissible."

"But—that's absurd!" Emma's blue eyes opened in shock. "I've given that man no indication that I am in the least bit interested in him. And why does Cole feel he can speak for me?"

Jane's heart lifted in spirit. She was relieved that Emma would not be encouraging the brash doctor. She moved closer to Emma. Close enough that she could whisper.

"Oh, Emma, promise me you won't see him, even if he comes asking for you. Tell Cole you will not receive him. Please. I couldn't bear it, dear. I would go mad imagining him touching you, stealing our time together, even for a moment."

Emma looked behind her and both ways before grabbing Jane by both arms are embracing her lightly, their breasts barely touching.

"I will never allow other hands to touch me that are not yours, Jane. My breasts, my lips, my scars, all hunger only for you." She smiled and planted a sweet kiss on Jane's forehead. "Do not fret, my love. Now, let me get back to our Henry before he finds something else to interest him besides a history examination." She paused as she pulled away. "I am truly sorry you won't be coming with us tomorrow. We shall plan another outing once the Brownes have mended."

Jane watched with unabashed lust as Emma glided along the veranda. The more time she spent with her, the more a distraction she became. Soon, it would all come to a head and Cole must know about their love. He must.

But still, Hannah Browne's accusations and hostility toward the woman she loved lingered and she could not brush the dark malady that gripped her soul. Something was wrong within Havenswood and she could still not break through the veil to see the root of the darkness.

***

That night, sleep was denied Jane once again. It was no longer easy to rest at Havenswood. The house was deep in grief. Jane could almost feel it closing in. She clung to the warmth and heat of her love for Emma Stiles. That was the only solid pillar of strength keeping her resolve. The corridors and hallways seemed to echo with impending doom. Outside on this night, the wind battered the old shutters, howled through the trees and tore at the faded face of Havenswood. But Emma had once brought light and joy to the house. Could she not work that magic again?

No, Jane could not find sleep. She was afraid to close her eyes for fear another calamity might strike.

Lord, please keep Emma safe.

It was the last prayer before exhaustion finally overtook her and sleep came like a thief in the blackness of night.

Chapter 11

When Jane came down from her room the following morning, she found Havenswood quiet and deserted.

Cole had taken the carriage and gone into town, according to Gabe Browne. Jane had come to bring tall glasses of lemonade and bowls of oatmeal to both Gabe and Hannah.

"How long have Emma and Henry been gone?" she asked Hannah, who winced at the mention of Emma's name.

"They left about an hour ago. Gone hiking to Greenroad Woods. Took Goldy with them. You should have seen Miss High and Mighty. Apparently, you pay her well enough to go out and buy herself those funny clothes she had for hiking. Humph."

"We pay her what she is worth, Hannah, like we do you and Gabe. And glad to do so. Did she mention when they would return?"

Gabe coughed. "Sundown, I suppose, Miss Havens. Greenroad Woods is mighty nice in the daylight. Lots of caves and gullies in there, you know."

Jane nodded. She knew. "I'll be doing some sewing on the veranda. Please call me if either of you need anything. I rather like waiting on you two for a change." She smiled, feeling much relieved and light of heart this morning.

A bright, pure sunlight caressed the front of the house, warming the porch and casting darts of sun off the white columns.

Jane, already having had a quick breakfast of oatmeal and juice, settled into a chair and neatly pressed out the pleats of her lilac taffeta dress. She inhaled the strong scent of green in the warm air and took an admiring glance at the neat, measured division of the Colonel's spruces lining the edges of the roadway. The livestock behind the barn noisily greeted the morning. For the first time in several days, Jane felt like it was the beginning of a good day. Perhaps the ugly days were in the past.

She tried to make some sense out of what had been happening at Havenswood, and the horrid accusations Hannah spoke against Emma. It hurt Jane's head too much to think of the puzzle. She shook her head to clear the thoughts away and took up the needle.

"Hello, there," a male voice called from nearby. Jane looked up, startled.

Dr. Rydell, wearing riding breeches and a tweed coat, cantered toward her.

"Doctor Rydell, was my brother expecting you or are you here for the Brownes?"

"Well, for the Brownes, of course." He slowed his pinto until it drew close to the portico where she sat. "The morning was so perfect that I thought I'd ride out without the doctor buggy." He chuckled. "May I pause to talk with you a moment before seeing Gabe and Hannah, Miss Havens?"

"Of course." What else could she say? She couldn't escape. "Cole is in town and Miss Stiles and Henry are off on a picnic hike." Jane hoped that maybe he would go away if Emma wasn't available.

He slid from the pony's back and tethered it to one of the portico posts.

"How are the Brownes coming along?"

"Quite well," Jane offered, wishing the conversation to end quickly.

He smiled wide. "Well, even though this is officially my day off, I thought it a perfect opportunity to look in on them before I leave."

The doctor seemed to linger and Jane was brought up to be a gracious hostess, whether a guest was likeable or not.

"Dr. Rydell, can I get you some refreshment? Coffee, lemonade, or a drink?"

He held up his hands. "Oh no, thank you. I've had breakfast with Peter Porter this morning. We discussed your family at some length."

Jane really didn't care who or what Dr. Rydell discussed. "How is Mr. Porter, the dear man?"

"As hearty as ever. I've seen less active men half his age."

Jane watched him and was suddenly struck with an idea. She remembered that on several occasions, he had mentioned that he had seen Emma before, in New York. If he would lend credibility to Emma, recognizing her as someone he actually knew, it might lead Hanna and even Cole to accept her and give her more respect. Yes, perhaps Dr. Rydell could prove useful after all.

"Miss Havens?" He was looking quizzically at her.

She smiled. "Dr. Rydell, I was wondering about something you have mentioned once or twice before in conversation."

"I suppose I've mentioned far too many things. Care to refresh my memory?"

"About Emma—I mean, Miss Stiles. I wondered if you were ever able to remember where you might had seen her before? What is it that makes her seem so familiar?"

His face became animated.

"Well, I probably shouldn't have mentioned that at all to anyone. You see, I was immediately struck by her amazing resemblance to a woman I once knew in passing. Of course, I knew it could not be the woman I had in mind. The circumstances involving that woman were very sad and unfortunate. I must admit, if I'd been pressed by your brother or Miss Stiles herself, I would have been quite embarrassed."

Jane frowned. "I'm not sure I understand."

Dr. Rydell cleared his throat. "You remember I said I had spent my childhood in New York. I also completed my schooling there. Shortly after finishing medical college, I started a small practice there. I wanted to work with the poor. I spent much time in the impoverished sections of the city tending to many of the transient poor population. I even went further beyond into the outskirts. It was there that I met and became acquainted with one of the most hauntingly beautiful women I have ever met."

Something about the story intrigued Jane. "Go on, doctor."

"This woman was pointed out to me one day by one of my medical assistants. I think her name was Collins and my keen interest and that of my colleagues was that she was in the first stages of consumption and with child—"

Jane gasped. "She was ill and pregnant?" She shook her head in disbelief. "How very sad."

"Yes. This woman was poor and in need of medical care, but she continued to work. She shuffled about with no one to care about her. I wanted to help but she'd shy away. In the end, she begged for someone to save her unborn child, having given up on her own life. As wasted as this woman was, she remained a superbly beautiful woman. In my conversation with Mr. Porter, I realized that it was that lady whom Miss Stiles reminded me of. There is quite an amazing resemblance, if truth be told."

Jane's hopes for some information to shed a more favorable light on her Emma faded, but the story of the beautiful but ill-fated woman was compelling.

"A terrible story. What happened to the lady?"

The doctor's eyes clouded. "She died. There was no saving her."

"Was there a family?"

"Her husband had died in the war. There was talk that she had a young child, but no one could prove anything. It's often that way with the very poor."

Jane sighed. "Oh, my!" she said, "Your story is so depressing. And her baby?"

"It was a boy. He perished with her."

Suddenly, the muscles in Jane's stomach twisted. Something was scrambling about in her mind. Something hidden in the shadows, not yet ready to see the light of day. It was jumbled like an incomplete puzzle. There was something in the story Dr. Rydell had just told— Something in the missing facts of his tale had sparked a fragile train of thought.

"About this story..." Jane paused, pursuing the persistent apparitions haunting her thoughts, "Have you mentioned it to Mr. Porter or Cole?"

He appeared surprised and shook his head.

"No, only Miss Stiles' uncanny resemblance to someone I had met in the past. Should I have kept that to myself?" He eyed her carefully.

Jane realized she had to be careful with the doctor.

"I don't really know. We'd love to know more about Miss Stiles. She is ultimately an employee—Henry's tutor—and I understand she came to us with high praises from her previous employers." She thought it an excellent response. The last thing she needed was someone other than Cole becoming suspicious about her interest in Emma. Jane believed everything her beloved had revealed about her past, but would it be so wrong to find out more from someone who may have known her in New York?

"Perhaps," she continued, "you could tell Mr. Porter about your strange, beautiful lady and we'll see what he says."

"Your wish is my command, Miss Havens, but what brings forth so much interest in a poor, unfortunate soul in New York from so long ago?"

"I think you already find the resemblance between our Miss Stiles and your woman as intriguing as I do. Or have I misread you, doctor?"

He broke into a wide smile. "Indeed. We shall both have our curiosity satisfied, then."

Jane glanced over his shoulder. The sun's rays stained the slanted roof of the barn just beyond a rich golden hue.

"Goodness," she said, "It's getting late."

Dr. Rydell smiled. "I won't keep you, Miss Havens. I'll be going as soon as I check in on Gabe and Hannah. Thank you for allowing me some of your time."

"Thank you for looking after them, doctor."

He disappeared into the house and Jane settled back into the chair, prepared to wait for Cole to return home. He should arrive before long. But in reality, she found that her gaze wandered west toward Greenroad Wood. She wondered how Henry was enjoying his picnic hike with Emma.

***

Long after Dr. Richard Rydell had ridden back toward Havens Falls, Cole walked into the family library, his cape a bit dusty and his dark hair damp from the long ride. Jane sat in the horsehair chair, her feet comfortably crossed on the ottoman, finishing her mending.

"Well, sister," he said with a touch of exhaustion, "where are the day's adventurers?"

Jane placed her sewing on her lap and checked the small mantle clock. She'd been so absorbed in her needlework, that she'd failed to notice the early evening shadows that had stealthily crept across the library walls and floor. It was 5:10.

"My goodness, I didn't realize it was so late."

"You mean they aren't back yet?"

"No," Jane replied. "They're probably having too much fun to worry about us worrying about them." She didn't want to panic yet or send Cole into a fit.

She jumped when he slammed his fist hard against his other hand. "That governess! This is too late for a woman and a boy to be marching about in a place like Greenroad Woods. Where the devil can they be?" He strode to the casement and swung open the shutters, staring out into the deepening darkness beyond.

"Emma will take good care of him," Jane said, through a nibble of worry that was already biting at her insides. "She promised they would be careful. And they have Goldy with them. He will find the way back if they do get waylaid."

"Emma." Cole repeated with obvious disdain. "I can no longer hold my tongue, Jane. You have an unnatural relationship with that woman." He pointed a finger at her. "Oh, yes, did you think I had not noticed? Has this obsession with her blinded you to reality? What do you really know about Miss Stiles? What do any of us really know? And yet, she is out there—" He waved a hand to the window. "He is only twelve years old. Children get frightened and confused in the dark woods, especially as the daylight falls away. Oh, why did I agree to such a fool thing?"

132

Jane was shocked at Cole's accusation. As much as she realized it was the perfect invitation to finally admit to him the depths of her true feelings for Emma, and Emma's for her, until she and Henry were safely back home at Havenswood, she thought it best to ignore it till then.

"Cole, please control yourself. I'm sure the are on the way back as we speak."

He snapped. "You're sure? Or maybe not." He turned abruptly toward the door. "I'd better mount up and go look for them before it gets pitch black. I won't be able to follow a trail then."

Jane tried to change the subject and bargained for time, hoping she was right and that in a few minutes, the pair would be walking through the front doors.

"Dr. Rydell came by today to check in on the Brownes."

"Or maybe he came by looking for your Miss Stiles."

Jane stood her ground, opting to say nothing to his comment and the meaning behind it. For a precious few seconds, Cole was stone quiet.

"Where in heaven's name could they be?" he yelled. "I will wait five minutes, then I shall most certainly go out in search of them. Miss Stiles had no business assuming she could stay out this late with Henry. If they are lost," Cole said with contempt, "Miss Stiles will have to answer to me personally."

As his voice faded in the room, a piercing scream, horrifying in its intensity and shocking in its anguish, rang through the air.

Cole's mouth twisted in surprise and Jane's eyes opened in shock. They both ran to the library door. Her heart was beating wildly. A frightening apparition greeted them as they reached the well-lighted foyer.

Emma stood in the entranceway. Her face turned down, staring at the floor. Emma shivered as if she were chilled. Her long, black hair was loose and tangled, trailing down her shoulders. Her breathing was labored and her chest rose and fell with fierce agitation.

Jane, not caring anymore about Cole's opinions, rushed to her and took her in her arms. Emma's clothes were wet and she swayed in Jane's arms, her eyes wild and pleading.

"I tried, Jane. I tried—but it was so dark and I lost my way...Oh, what have I done?" She began to weep on Jane's chest.

"Emma, what happened?" Jane searched her face.

Cole immediately came and grabbed Emma by her shoulders, barreling Jane out of the way, his eyes blazing.

"Henry....where is Henry?"

"Cole, stop it!" Jane cried out. "Can't you see she's terrified."

He ignored Jane's plea and continued to shake Emma.

"Tell me, now, in God's name, where is my brother?"

"He is lost!" screamed Emma. "Lost. In one of the caves. Both he and Goldy are lost. I tried calling for them, but they were gone. But hurry, Mr. Havens. Go, before it's too late. It's getting so dark, so dark—"

"You fool!" Cole raged as he released her. "You careless, stupid fool. I swear to you, if anything happens to Henry—"

Without saying another word, Cole ran out the door, his cape flying behind him. Jane began to utter silent prayers. Suddenly, Emma rushed away from her and out the door of the library. Behind Jane, sounding far away, like a buoy at sea, Hannah Browne's bell began to ring frantically.

Jane wanted to run after Emma, kiss her fiercely and tell her everything would be all right, but she could not abandon an injured Hannah Browne.

"Oh, what has happened to Havenswood?" she moaned out loud.

If something has happened to Henry, how will we ever bear it?

Chapter 12

Since the day Emma had come into Havenswood with her icy beauty, mysterious trunk and fierce eyes, time had lost all meaning for Jane. She had fallen hopelessly in love and learned of ecstasy she had never dreamed of.

But the reality was that the longer it took Cole to return with her little brother, the more depressed she became. She dared not give voice to what she feared the most, that Cole would not find Henry or that Henry was dead.

Hannah was beside herself to know what tragedy had befallen the Havens yet again. The older woman had lived too long and had an uncanny ability to sense impending tragedy in the air to not know something had indeed occurred.

Hannah had purposefully continued ringing the bell at her bedside until Jane, nerves at their breaking point, came to see her. When she broke the news to her, Hannah nearly choked with acidic words aimed against Emma.

"I rue the day that woman came to Havenswood! She has cursed this house. Oh, my poor Henry. Out there in those dark, lonely woods all by his lonesome. How I detest that woman. I tell you, Miss Jane, I could see her dead and not shed a tear."

Jane loved Hannah dearly. She'd been like a mother to her and she respected her greatly, but she would not stand there and allow her to speak such vile words about Emma.

"Hannah, please. Henry does have Goldy with him," Jane begged.

"She's right. Keep your tongue still, Hannah," Gabe said sternly, noticing Jane's weakened state. "Christian women don't speak like that in times like these."

"No, Gabe Browne, I'll not be silent. I warned you it would come to no good. And now the thing's done. A fool dog is no help to that boy in the wilderness. That witch shall be the death of our boy, mark my—" Hannah only stopped, her voice fading, when she saw the surge of tears in Jane's eyes, spilling down her cheeks.

"Lord forgive me, Miss Jane," she said gently. "I am so sorry—"

There was nothing left to say. Jane left running from the room, tears nearly blinding her. She closed her ears to Hannah's entreaties to come back. Hannah did not ring her bell again.

Jane waited in the library. She couldn't go to Emma in such a state. It would only upset her again. No, she would wait for Cole and Henry and Goldy to come running through the library doors.

Even though it was a warm night, Jane was cold. She wrapped her shawl about her shoulders and sat down carefully in Cole's chair. She sighed, wishing to be in Emma's bed, warm and loved. But Jane sat instead, watching the flames of the candles and the lamps dance and burn. Time, measured by the Swiss clock, seemed to tick in an unnaturally slow rhythm. She sat still, staring without seeing, at the empty and cold fireplace.

Henry. Henry. Please come home safe.

***

Jane barely made it through the next several hours of her life. And then Cole suddenly appeared in the doorway to the library, as if he had never gone out at all. As if nothing were wrong. As if Henry lay asleep in his bed upstairs, safe and sound. Her eyes riveted on Cole. He stood like some apparition out of the night. His cape was torn and stained with mud and who knew what else. His drawn face was ghostly pale; desperation gleaming in his eyes.

He stood helpless, shoulders drooped, every inch of his body a proclamation of defeat. They stared at each other, silent, wallowing in fear.

"Cole—"

"Jane...I...couldn't find him."

She struggled to stifle the cry that threatened to erupt from her throat.

"Jane, he's lost out there in all that darkness. We can do nothing now but wait until morning and gather more men from Havens Falls."

Jane fought to control the rising panic in her chest.

"Surely, Cole, we can do something now. Ride to town. Tell the sheriff. Get Peter Porter and Dr. Rydell. We mustn't let the dark hinder our search. We can bring torches, lamps, candles...anything. For God's sake, Cole, don't just stand there reproaching yourself. Think of Henry! We must act now."

His eyes flashed in a rage. "Think of Henry? I have done nothing but think of our little brother for all these hours. I have worried myself nearly out of my mind!"

He stumbled past her toward the liquor cabinet. "I need a drink."

"No, not now. Please."

"Why not now? I can't think of a better time."

He fumbled with the latticed glass and wood door of the cabinet. The bottles clinked as he searched for his favorite brandy bottle.

Jane was near the end of her rope. She had to retain even a seed of hope in her soul.

"Perhaps Henry and Goldy will find their way back. Goldy is a great guide. That dog knows those woods so well—"

"Of course he does," Cole answered cynically, "but not an unexplored cave. I will wring that little scamp's neck when I get my hands on him." He swung his glass to his lips and drained it in one gulp.

"Cole, you cannot keep that up all night."

"Get out, Jane," he rasped. "Don't you dare stand there in judgment of my weaknesses, not when you have exposed your near blasphemous ones yourself, sister. I choose to spend my time waiting in the only way that is tolerable to me."

Jane felt any softness she'd felt for her brother dry up and whither away to a hard, firm resolve. She straightened her back and stared at him coldly.

"Cole Havens," she said with an icy, even voice, "You go ahead and drown yourself in that foul liquid if you like, but I will not sit still within these walls as long as Henry is out there lost in those woods. I'm riding to Havens Falls and find Mr. Porter and Dr. Rydell. I am thoroughly ashamed of you. If the Colonel were alive, I am sure he would be as well."

"I told you to get out," he growled again, his back turned away. "You will never understand."

"You're right," she said, sweeping past him, head held high. "And I'm certain nobody in the world would understand how you can drown your sorrows in that swill while our little brother could be in mortal danger."

139

Jane couldn't control her anger. She slammed the doors violently behind her before she allowed the tears to erupt from her eyes. Teardrops streaming, she ran into the hall closet, her heels clattering across the polished floor. She dragged out her riding cape and a broad-brimmed bonnet and put them on quickly. There wasn't a moment to waste.

The ride to Havens Falls would be windy and hazardous in the dark, thanks to the clinging brambles and low-hanging trees on the roadway. She could not let those fears interfere with her one goal. She had to get to town and alert anyone and everyone to the plight of her little brother.

The Brownes would have to fend for themselves or get Cole to acknowledge them. There was a less than slim chance of that ever happening.

She could not spend the night within the walls of Havenswood while Henry was still lost somewhere in a cave in Greenroad Woods. It was simply unthinkable. Cole had been right about one thing—daylight would be better to conduct a search, but that was hours away. What could happen before then? Jane shuddered when she contemplated the black bears that were now coming out of hibernation, and the little brown bats that hung from the grotto ceilings.

As she rushed across the verandah, heading for the barn, she became aware of the darkness pressing in around her—the thick, oppressive moisture that came with the blackness of night. The moon kept playing hide and seek with fast moving clouds. She had a difficult time finding her way to the stables without a lantern to guide her.

Suddenly, Jane was consumed with the hopelessness of her ride. A grim sense of loss overwhelmed her. It felt so futile, really. A boy lost in the vast, rambling forest dotted with a dozen dark caves, masses of trees and bushes, fast-running streams, and the lake Henry had toppled into before. How could they hope to find her little brother?

She would not allow herself to succumb to negative thinking. She physically shook herself free of her dark imaginations and sought out the black gelding, Shadow, saddling him with haste. The horse, familiar to her, nuzzled her and neighed softly. Jane rubbed him lovingly.

She sobbed to herself as her fingers worked with the cinches.

God, please, keep him safe.

She repeated the prayer to herself as she rode out at a gallop.

Chapter 13

*H*avens Falls had not seen a tragedy in several years, since Tim John's ten- year-old Toby had fallen off Mt. Bearhook and died on the rocks below. The town had been shocked and went into mourning after that terrible event. No one had forgotten it. So when Jane rode into town at a gallop, waking Peter Porter and also Dr. Richard Rydell, the saloons were abuzz and many took to the street to engage in speculation.

Mr. Porter had been fast asleep in his room at Wilkins House when the bustle and voices reached his ears. Before he could latch the last button on his vest, someone was pounding on his door. Jane Havens and Dr. Rydell swept by him into the room.

"What is going on?" the old lawyer grumbled. "Is the church on fire again?" He eyed Jane. "Miss Havens, what are you doing here?"

"Miss Havens rode into town just a short while ago," Rydell glanced at Jane. "She found me in my office. Henry is in trouble again."

"Henry is lost in Greenroad Woods, Mr. Porter," Jane explained. "Cole spent a few hours looking for him, but we fear he may have wandered into one of the caves. I was desperate and didn't know what to do. Cole believes we should wait till morning, but I do not agree."

Porter tried to focus his sleepy eyes. He was still trying to wake up.

"Henry? Lost? Good Lord, how did that happen?"

"Emma—" Jane stopped. "Miss Stiles wanted to reward him for progressing so well in his studies, so they went on a picnic hike. He'd wanted to go hiking for some time. She came back without him, after dark."

"Good Lord," Peter Porter murmured again.

"Peter, in light of all that has happened at Havenswood recently, do you have a few moments to discuss a few new details I've discovered about Miss Stiles?"

The old lawyer cleared his throat. "Is this pertaining to our previous conversation about the woman?"

"It is."

"Yes, yes of course," Mr. Porter muttered. "But let's get the sheriff to round up some townsfolk to join a search party out to Greenroad Woods tonight."

The doctor glanced at Jane. "You should join us as well, Miss Havens. It might answer some of the questions you had this morning."

Jane, intrigued by the sudden interest in Emma by Dr. Rydell, couldn't dream of not joining them.

***

Jane sat in the weathered client chair across from Mr. Porter in his law office. Dr. Rydell sat next to her atop a wooden stool Porter had pulled from his law library room.

Porter puffed on a cigar, a grim look on his normally pleasant face.

"Let us all hope and pray Sheriff Marley and the rescue party will find Henry and Goldy and bring them home safe."

"I have never stopped praying," Jane added. "But if Dr. Rydell can please hurry," she glanced at the doctor, "I wish to ride back to Havenswood as quickly as possible."

"As do we all, Miss Havens," Dr. Rydell said. He cast a serious look at Mr. Porter. "Peter, you know I have referenced several times the strong resemblance between Emma Stiles and someone I have seen before. Would you indulge me in a few quick questions?"

The portly Mr. Porter nodded. "Proceed," he said, taking strong puffs from the cigar.

Dr. Rydell took a deep breath and Jane gripped the arms of the old wooden chair tightly. Rydell looked at her intently.

"And Miss Havens, please don't take my questions as an affront on the integrity of your father. I am not just a curiosity seeker. Please bear me out."

She nodded slowly, not sure she understood what he was trying to imply.

"Peter, when Colonel Vincent Havens died, how was his estate disposed of? I mean, was there a will?"

"What does my father have to do with any of this?" Jane straightened her back, slightly disturbed with Dr. Rydell's line of questions. He had no right to bring her father's name into this.

Dr. Rydell threw up his hands. "I mean no disrespect, Miss Havens, as I have said. Please allow me to complete my thoughts. Please indulge me a few minutes more."

Mr. Porter eyed Jane. "Miss Jane, I don't believe the good doctor means any harm." He looked back at Dr. Rydell. "There was a will, of course. I drew it up myself. The Colonel left the estate to Cole as his eldest, since Jane and young Henry were little more than children. Is that all you wanted to know?" He looked at the doctor with curiosity.

"No," Dr. Rydell said. "Were there any documents, letters, mementos, private items?"

Porter narrowed his eyes and Jane rose to her feet, eyes blazing. "How could you waste our time while my little brother is in trouble out there in those dark woods? You disappoint me, doctor. Our family trusted you."

Mr. Porter got up and reached over to Jane.

"Now, calm down, Miss Jane. Let's give the good doctor a chance to explain what this is all about. I trust the Sheriff to search every inch of the woods. We can join them shortly." He smiled warmly at her.

If Jane wasn't so fond of Mr. Porter and appreciative of all his help with Havenswood, she would have walked out. But something inside—something insistent, told her to stay put.

Once Jane and Peter Porter sat back down, the lawyer stared at the doctor.

"Now Richard, I know you come from New York. Your father was one of my best friends. I suppose you, like everyone else, has heard the talk and the rumors about Colonel Havens. All of it. At one time, it was like a raging fire. It was quite a story. Many of these people are dead now. What are you driving at, son?"

"Yes, Doctor Rydell, why are you wasting our time?" Jane said. She began to feel sick to her stomach. Had the doctor remembered something about Emma?

There was an uncomfortable moment of silence.

"I wish I knew," Dr. Rydell murmured. "both of you have heard me mention that I thought I had seen Emma Stiles before. Just recently, in a conversation with Miss Havens here, I realized why she looked so familiar to me."

"Go on, Richard."

"When I was out to see Miss Havens and check on the Brownes, I mentioned that I had known a strange, beautiful woman—a reluctant patient—when I was a young medical student. She was dying of consumption but was with child." He eyed Peter Porter seriously. "Well, Peter, that woman was an older, even more beautiful image of Miss Stiles—"

He broke off his narrative because his friend, Mr. Porter, had squashed his cigar into the ashtray, his old hands knotted into fists.

Jane watched Mr. Porter, confused. What angered him? What kind of puzzle was Dr. Rydell trying to piece together? Could it even be connected to her own puzzle? Sitting in a musty old law office discussing a sad woman from long ago, while Henry might have returned home was not where she wished to be.

Her thoughts were interrupted by Peter Porter.

"Do you know the full story about Colonel Hastings and the woman he was said to have dallied with on his way back to Havenswood that last month of the war?" Porter glared at Rydell.

The doctor nodded hesitantly. "It is a legendary bit of gossip around New York. My father never spoke of it to me, but I heard things when I was a young man. Later, when I went to see this woman, I did not associate her with the stories I had heard. But—"

"Yes, yes," Porter grumbled. "It was true enough—" He paused and looked at Jane. His face softened. "I'm sorry, Miss Jane, that we're discussing this unfortunate affair in front of you."

"I'm no longer a child, Mr. Porter. I have heard them all at great length and can memorize every dirty bit of gossip—"

"It is no gossip, dear child," Porter sighed. "And I think you realize that as much as your have chosen not to believe it." His eyes were warm and loving as he spoke to her.

Jane mustered a smile at the old lawyer then looked at Dr. Rydell.

"You told me the baby did not live, Dr. Rydell. Is it possible that the dead infant was my baby brother?"

"I am deeply sorry, Miss Havens. You are right. That lovely woman did not survive and neither did her unborn son—"

"Dear God!" Peter Porter exclaimed, his fist slamming the desk so hard it rattled a metal tub of ink so that it nearly sloshed its contents across the desk toward Jane.

She jumped back. "Mr. Porter, whatever is the matter?"

"All those years, I've wondered about those letters. Those secret letters the Colonel entrusted to me." He almost spoke to himself, but then his gaze shifted from Jane to Dr. Rydell.

"Letters?" Jane asked, suddenly ever more intrigued.

"Yes, your father left a stack of maybe six letters and—" Again, he slammed his other fist down hard on the desk. The ink remained settled in the ink well.

Jane's heart began to race and her chest felt tight.

"Are you meaning to suggest that there really is some connection to that woman and Emma and the Colonel?" Inside, Jane's world was beginning to tilt sideways.

"Suggest? Suggest?" Peter Porter was stuttering now.

"Peter," Dr. Rydell said, "the woman's name was Collins. Do you think there might be anything in Colonel Havens's letters or possessions that might shed more light on this?"

Jane thought the room was spinning. It was getting difficult to breathe. All she wanted now was to be back home at Havenswood, lying beside Emma and Henry safe in his room with Goldy lying beside his bed. She wished desperately that this was all a nightmare and she would wake up soon....soon. She did not want to peel away the veil from the mysterious woman that could have been an exact image of her beloved Emma. Would Jane even be able to understand or truly mourn a little brother that she never knew? She feared only horrors would be revealed. Some secrets were meant to stay hidden, weren't they? What had she started when she invited the doctor to help her uncover the truth?

"Proof. We need proof—" Porter muttered to himself.

"There must be something, Peter. There are always untidy little things that we leave behind when we pass. Residue. Those letters, a postcard, a photograph—"

Mr. Porter suddenly looked at him as if he had uttered a blasphemy. His face broke out in amazement.

"Of course. The miniature!"

Jane inhaled a deep breath and her knuckles turned white as she grasped the chair even tighter.

"What miniature, Mr. Porter? There was no miniature that I remember in father's things that you gave to Cole."

"No. Let me explain. I gave all the important papers to your brother. I didn't want those left here in this office for fear of fire..." He paused, his face deep in thought. "Your father, my dear, left instructions privately for me in his will. Certain things were to remain with me and away from his children..." He paused again, looking away from Jane. "Cole, of course, was to have everything else."

Jane knew perfectly well what Mr. Porter was having trouble admitting. As painful as it was, the reality was that her father had had secrets. He had conducted an affair with a beautiful, sad and sick woman in New York. Now those skeletons were floating out of the closet with a vengeance.

"Now let me think," he said. "Where did I put away the miniature and those letters?" Porter placed his fingers on his temples and massaged, as if the very act would produce the answers he sought.

"Are they in your safe?" Dr. Rydell asked.

Porter waved his hand in the air and shook his head. "No. Safes were made to be broken into. They are temptations of the devil." He frowned. "I haven't seen that miniature painting in nearly a decade." He glanced at Jane and then away. "The Colonel had it on him when he arrived back in Havens Falls." He paused again. "You must understand, Miss Jane, that the Colonel acted as if it wasn't a very important item. He gave it to me, saying merely that it was too beautiful to throw away. Oh, I am getting too old to even remember what that little locket with the painting looks like, or even where I've put it away—"

"Please, Peter, try to remember," Rydell insisted. He glanced at Jane, who sat silent and still. "Miss Havens, it may answer some of the questions we have about your governess and also about your father."

Jane could not find her voice. It was suddenly stifled in the dusty, cluttered office.

"I really don't think this is the time or the place to do this," she finally said quietly.

Peter Porter grunted. "Confound it, now where could I—" Abruptly, his face beamed. He slapped his leg. "Well, trust an old fool, will you. I knew I would remember. And it couldn't be in a finer or safer place in the entire world for such a potentially damaging memento."

"Well, where is it, Peter?" Dr. Rydell asked impatiently.

"No one would ever guess. Those letters are there too. Come, we'll all go fetch them before heading back to Havenswood. No time to waste."

Jane sat still, not able to move. Part of her didn't want to follow them. She didn't want to drag out her father's tainted past for the condemnation of all in Havens Falls. And more importantly, she feared that all of this was

149

going to touch Emma. She knew all she needed or wanted to know about her lover.

"Where are those letters and the miniature, Mr. Porter?" she asked.

"Why, in the Havens Falls town library."

"The what?" Dr. Rydell looked surprised.

"We have a Civil War collection there. The spoils of war, so to speak, locked beneath glass. The miniature is part of the display of one Colonel Lockley of the Union Army, Pennsylvania." Porter grinned. "It seemed like the most ideal place in 1867 to bury the locket. No one really knows much about Colonel Lockley, let alone come to see his mementos. I had no use for it. The letters are there too, somewhere in a box. I had forgotten those things until you brought it all back tonight."

"We should hurry, then, Mr. Porter," Jane said, desperate to be back at Havenswood, away from this madness. "If the library is still open—"

"Oh, no, child, it isn't open. Miss Dinton closes up quite early. Not many visit, you see." He scratched his chin, deep in thought, then turned to Jane. "You know, it suddenly occurs to me that there was an inscription of some sort on the back of that locket."

"An inscription?" Dr. Rydell asked.

Jane held her breath. "What kind of inscription?"

"A name. A woman's name."

"Then we'd best go and rouse your Miss Dinton, the librarian," Jane said. "I cannot wait here much longer. I must get back to Cole and Havenswood. Henry might be back."

Porter nodded. "Fine, then. Miss Dinton will be furious and knowing her wagging tongue, everyone in Havens Falls will know about our strange request come morning, but let's get it done, then."

Jane followed them slowly. Her body felt deflated, like a balloon that was losing air and falling fast to the hard earth below.

Chapter 14

*T*he locket was startling.

It was a miniature painting on an oval wafer of porcelain, framed in precious gold. The portrait was of a young woman whose radiant beauty would surely have taken away the breath of every man who saw her.

Jane held it in her palm with the chain wrapped about her slim fingers. Beside her, Peter Porter was busy making apologies to Miss Dinton for waking her from her sleep in the middle of the night. The prune-faced, gaunt woman stood half-awake, a bitter look on her face, arms folded.

As Jane held on to the table beside her to steady herself, her knuckles turned white. Beads of sweat formed on her forehead as she realized the woman in the painting looked just like Emma.

"Yes," Dr. Rydell said as he studied the locket in her hand, "that is the Collins woman. I would swear to it. I have no doubt."

Was the room getting dim or was it Jane's imagination? She was having trouble breathing as her thoughts became jumbled. The woman in the miniature obviously was not Emma, yet the likeness was alarming. But a troubling question loomed like a malignant cloud. What did her father, the Colonel, have to do with this woman? And was this woman related to Emma? Emma was never specific in her stories about her mother. Could this be her mother's portrait? Jane took a deep breath of musty air and her stomach churned.

"You are quite right, Richard," Mr. Porter removed the locket from her possession and examined the reverse side. "There is the name on the back plate—Amanda Collins. There is no mistake."

Jane found her voice as she continued to stare at the miniature.

"Dr. Rydell, did you not mention to me that this woman, this Amanda Collins, had another child, besides the unborn she lost? Do you know if it was a girl or boy?"

The doctor furrowed his eyebrows in thought.

"Talk was pretty sketchy...some said a son while others said a daughter. I have no idea if that was true or not."

Jane staggered back and Dr. Rydell reached out to steady her.

"Are you all right, Miss Havens?"

Jane put her hand on her forehead. "I'm fine, doctor. It's just a bit stuffy in here."

Peter Porter continued to study the necklace with interest.

"Collins," he mumbled. "Good Lord, Richard, look at the letters in this name!" He exclaimed, his eyes open in surprise. "The letters."

"Mr. Porter," Jane asked in a near whisper, what does all this have to do with my father? Why did he have this locket? I must know for certain."

He took her hand and held it. "My dear, come with me and we will piece this together, God willing." He turned to Miss. Dinton who stood yawning in the back of the room. "Quickly, Miss. Dinton, take us to that box I left with you that contained Colonel's letters."

The woman looked at him with a blank stare.

153

"Wake up, woman! This is important. Where do you keep your boxes with letters and documents?"

She glared at him, a scowl on her face. "You needn't get nasty, Peter Porter. I know where the box is. It's in the storage closet in the office out back."

Miss Dinton's bleak little office in the even bleaker library was lit only by a candelabra sitting on her desk. Jane wanted to flee from the suffocating room. She knew—she felt in her heart, that only misery waited in that box. The haunting face of the woman in the portrait remained imprinted in her head forever. It surely had to be Emma's mother. But how did it all connect to the Colonel? Were the answers all here, and if they were, could she stand to know the truth?

She felt out of control, like the world was crumbling around her.

"Here they are." Mr. Porter had opened a white box merely marked in heavy pencil: "Colonel." He dug out a think stack of letters wrapped with string. Jane noticed a thin band of yellowing surrounding the edges. Age and mildew were eating away at the paper fibers.

Dr. Rydell pulled out a pocket knife and cut the string. Porter eyed Jane as Dr. Rydell pried open the first envelope. Jane moved to stand beside him, looking at the address on the front of the envelope. *Colonel Vincent Havens, Havenswood, Havens Falls, Pennsylvania* was written in a neat, rather elegant hand in black ink. There was no return address.

She stepped back and turned away. Suddenly, the feeling that she was a voyeur to something obscene—something that would bring ghosts back to Havenswood, overwhelmed her.

Both Dr. Rydell and Porter each held a letter, intensely reading.

"Well I'll be—" Mr. Porter said slowly. He stared at Jane who still stood with her back turned. His mouth opened but no words came out. He simply continued to stare at the letter .

"This letter is filled with hate and threats." Rydell's voice was excited as he peered at the letter Porter held. "How about yours?"

"No, Richard, not this one. See here, the post mark is earlier than yours."

Jane suddenly moved forward, head spinning in the darkened room.

"May I see that letter, please?"

"Of course, Miss Jane." He passed her the yellowed letter, eyeing her with concern. "It isn't tasteful, Miss Jane."

"The truth often isn't," Jane said, her gaze on the handwriting before her.

January 18, 1866

To Colonel Havens,
I was told you were an good man. My mother insisted I respect you but I have my doubts now. My mother is Amanda Collins. Do you even remember her? She is very sick. Very sick. She is carrying your baby. Your baby is also sick inside her. My mother does not know I am writing you. We are hungry and my mother needs food for two and she needs medicines and doctor care. You said you were a well to do gentleman. Please help my mother. Please send us enough for medicine and for food too.

The letter wasn't signed, yet the formation of each letter, the spacing and the big "C" in Colonel seemed somehow familiar to Jane.

"May I see that other letter, Dr. Rydell?"

The doctor had already moved on and opened some of the other letters. He handed the first one to Jane. It was the same handwriting, but the words, the letters, seemed angry, hurried. Even the ink was splotchy, as if the letter writer were pressing down in a fit of fury.

October 5, 1866

The Great and Mighty Colonel Havens,

You disgust me. You and your family live in your mansion while my mother died calling out your name. You never wrote. Never came. You never cared. I curse you and your name and your family. I will fan the flames of vengeance in my heart until my dying days. I shall see that you and yours pay my price.

Dr. Rydell shook his head as he put down the last of the letters. "I'm sorry, Miss Havens, that you had to see these." He lowered his gaze from her.

Mr. Porter pulled a white handkerchief and wiped his forehead. He shook his head slowly.

"My dear child, I am so sorry you had to be subjected to this..." He paused, taking a deep breath. "Your father was not an evil man. You must know this. He did what he thought best for his family, to protect you and Cole and Henry."

"He protected us by turning his back on the dying mother of his unborn child? His own blood? What makes us different or better than that little baby inside Amanda Collins?" Jane's stomach hurt and her heart felt betrayed. Had any of them really known the man they always called the Colonel? Could she ever imagine her father had been so ugly inside?

156

She held her head high as she looked directly at Mr. Porter and Dr. Rydell.

"My father abandoned that woman he chose to love. The he abandoned his own unborn child, a baby he created in lust. I am sure he never gave a moment's consideration to her other child. He ignored her pleas, and that is an abomination. I am only his daughter. I cannot make reparation or excuses for my father's sins." Jane knew that if she did not leave now, she would break down.

Mr. Porter took her arm. "Of course, my dear, each of us can only take responsibility for our own deeds. No one is asking—"

"Look, Peter, Miss Havens," Dr. Rydell interrupted, "We're missing a very dangerous and pressing concern here." He held up the stack of letters. "These letters were obviously written by Amanda Collins's other child. I posit that there is the extreme possibility that your governess, Miss Havens, could be that daughter. Think about this." He held up the miniature locket. "Look at the picture. The likeness. What if Emma Stiles is Amanda Collins's daughter? She knew where to find Havenswood. The accidents at Havenswood began after she arrived at the house—"

"Dear God—" Mr. Porter gasped.

"No!" Jane had barely screamed the word before she grabbed the miniature from the table and rushed from the room. She ran through the door of the Havens Falls Library as if a wild wind buffeted her from behind, and ran, tears streaming down her cheeks, letter still grasped tightly in her fingers.

"Emma!" she called into the night.

She knew it. She knew it deep down in the depths of her heart. Emma was Amanda Collins's daughter. Had she really come to exact the hate and the vengeance she wrote of with such anger in those letters? Had Emma betrayed her too by professing love only to gain access to the family in order to carry out her promise of revenge? No. Emma loved her. Jane knew it with every fiber of her being. She had to get to Havenswood.

"Miss Jane, wait!" Peter Porter and Dr. Rydell were running to catch up with her. If they reached Havenswood before her, Cole would hear only the worst from their lips. She would not wait for them.

Jane ran hard, lifting her skirt high to jump quickly atop Shadow. She ran past a group of men standing in the street, nearly running into one of them. They tried to slow her down.

"Miss Havens, are you all right?" One man she recognized as Clement Owens, owner of the goods store.

Another man shouted, "We'll be right behind you , miss. We're gathering more townsfolk to help search for Henry!"

She didn't stop. She couldn't. The few people who had gathered thus far stared at her and began talking amongst themselves. Soon after, Porter and Dr. Rydell followed far behind her

Jane reached Shadow, who was tied at the post near Wilkins House. Without even looking behind her, she untied the reins, flung herself over and atop the saddle, grabbed the reins, and nudged the gelding into a trot.

Jane didn't know or care if Mr. Porter or the doctor were following her. She imagined they would, letters in hand. She had to reach Emma and Cole first. She silently prayed that Cole would be sober. Inside, Jane felt as if the flames of destruction were consuming her. Her world had disintegrated in one night. What awaited her on the other side?

She rode Shadow hard through the dark road heading out of Havens Falls and up to Havenswood, the wind baying at her back like the hounds of Hell.

"Dear God, how many trials and tribulations must I endure?" Her voice died in the blackness of the night.

Chapter 15

On the dark road back to Havenswood, Jane ran across one of the men from the search party. Heart joyful that perhaps Henry had been found, she reined in Shadow.

"Has my brother been found?"

The man shook his head. "No, Miss Havens, but we've got men spread out all over these woods. We'll find him. I just gotta run back for more oil for the lantern." He held up the darkened lamp.

Jane bit her lip to prevent herself from crying. Even with the scattered light of the lamps and torches lighting up Greenroad Woods like fireflies, Jane thought the woods dark, lonely and howling with a fierce wind.

Without another word, she took off in a gallop toward the road into Greenroad Woods. She was soon at Rock Lake, the water like a giant, wet glistening jewel, and beyond, the dense, crowded trees. The rocks surrounding the lake skulked like grey figures ready to pounce. Where could she go next? Desperation and fear gnawed at her, the realization of total futility too much to bear.

He's here. I know he is.

"Henry!" She screamed into the wall of darkness, fear overwhelming her. "Henry. Follow my voice. It's Jane. I'm taking you home. Let Goldy guide you.

Her voice rebounded off the rocks and rattled around through the trees, catching in the wind. There was no answer.

The woods, silent and unyielding, seemed to wait with ghostly anticipation. Jane peered deep into the dark, straining her eyes.

"Henry!" she shouted again.

His name crashed against the rocks at the shoreline and tumbled into the water.

"He's here, dear God, I know he's in there," Jane whispered in the gloom. She could see some of the bright lights from the lamps and torches moving toward her in the darkness ahead. Only a deaf man could not have heard her screams.

"Henry!" This time, her tears sounded in her screams. "It's Jane. Please answer me! I'm going to take you home. Follow my voice, Henry."

Sheriff Marley and some of his posse, dark shadows mounted with flaming torches and lanterns, came closer. Jane could not let her hope fade. She would not be defeated this easily. But Henry should have heard her cries by now. Her throat was hoarse from yelling. She felt certain he was within earshot of her voice if he was in the cave she suspected he might be in. It was the largest cave in Greenroad. It was the cave everyone visited and the only one large enough for two or more people and a dog.

Just as the group of men neared, a small shadow darted into view, seemingly out of nowhere. Her heart stopped beating. Following behind that, a larger shadow appeared. They both stood outlined against the moonlit night sky.

"Over there!" One of the men pointed.

Before the men could shout out in triumph or fire a shot, Goldy jumped out and Henry stumbled forward, running for Jane from the blackness.

161

"Janey! Janey!"

He flung himself into her arms, Goldy jumping up and down against her. Jane's heart burst with joy. Henry embraced her tightly, his tears smearing her own. She cried without restraint. Henry was safe. Safe!

Shots were fired into the air and the thunder of men rejoicing filled the forest.

"Henry, Henry," Jane repeated, wiping the dirt from her little brother's face. "How did you get lost?"

"We were playing hide-and-seek and Miss Stiles, she went away while I hid. I waited and waited for her to come back, but she never did and then it got so dark, Janey. I was too scared to go through the woods alone. Oh, please, Janey, please take me home—" He was shaking in her arms and suddenly went limp.

She felt a strong hand on her shoulder.

"Miss Havens, the boy has fainted." Sheriff Marley said. "Best let me take him."

"Oh, my Henry," she whispered.

The sheriff lifted Henry from her and cradled him gently in his big arms. Around them, the darkness had melted away. The forest and lake were suddenly alive with burning torches and more men with lamps.

Jane rose, shaky and swaying. Henry was safe, but she knew that at Havenswood, the storm was only beginning.

***

Sheriff Marley and the search party had taken their leave at the fork of the hilltop. At least all those good men of Havens Falls were going home to their families. Jane and Cole were to be in their debt for the rest of their lives.

The Sheriff had told her he would be back in the morning to question Emma, and have a talk with Cole.

Jane would not allow him to pressure Emma, but she had been too tired to fight him off this night.

Only a solitary light burned in the library window at Havenswood as Jane and a sleeping Henry galloped onto the gravel road leading to the entry gate.

Cole. Still up, drinking himself into oblivion.

Jane dismounted and helped the half-awake Henry to the ground. Goldy bounded ahead to the door. The sound of squealing springs reached her ears. As the sound grew nearer, she finally saw the riding lanterns of Dr. Rydell's rig. Both he and Peter Porter looked grim and solemn, but when they saw Henry with her, their faces lit up with joy and relief.

"Thank God," Mr. Porter said wearily. "The boy is safe."

Dr. Rydell bounced from his carriage and rushed forward to join Jane and Henry.

"Miss Havens, Henry, are you both all right?"

"Where was he?" Porter asked, peering at Henry's bleary-eyed face.

"He was in the big cave by Rock Lake." Jane was tired and exasperated.

"I'll make sure to look him over in the morning after he's rested to check for bruises or bites. We don't know what's in those caves," Dr. Rydell added, eyeing the quickly slumping Henry.

Jane realized that both Dr. Rydell and Mr. Porter here meant they had come to confront Emma and Cole about the secrets discovered tonight. She looked at both of them through tired eyes.

"Couldn't you have waited till the morning for this?"

"No, Miss Jane," Mr. Porter said shaking his head. "I think you understand our reasons for being here, and the severity of the situation cannot wait until the morning. Please understand that our Miss Stiles could be the author of those letters and if so, she is a very real danger to you and your entire family."

Jane suddenly remembered the unsigned letter she had crumpled and stuffed into her skirt pocket as she'd run out of the Havens Falls Library. She couldn't let Mr. Porter or Dr. Rydell know that she'd noticed a slight resemblance in the handwriting, especially the big letter "C" in the word Colonel.

"Let's go inside," Jane finally said, urging the tired Henry along. "I'd like to put Henry to bed."

Mr. Porter nodded. "Indeed, let's talk inside after we've seen to the boy."

They waited in the foyer while Jane escorted Henry to his room and set up fresh water in the table basin to wash his face and hands. While he did that, she searched his desk for the cutout paper Christmas tree that Emma had shown him how to make. She had written "Merry Christmas" across the tree—with a big letter "C."

Jane found it in the top drawer. She grabbed it quickly and kissed Henry goodnight before she closed the door behind her. Her heart beat like a wild, galloping stallion.

Jane leaned against Henry's door and unfolded the mysterious letter that had been sent to her father by a pleading young child afraid for her mother's life. But was she ready for the truth? Below in the foyer of Havenswood, two men were ready to bring accusations against Emma Stiles. They came demanding to know if she was the one cursing Havenswood, and the cause of the dark things occurring to all within these walls. No, Jane would not believe that Emma, her beloved—the woman who had made passionate love to every inch of her body, the woman who had pledged her love in every way she could—was responsible for the accidents plaguing their household. But what if she was? Could not a soul find love and change her ways?

Jane looked at the ornate cursive flowing through the yellowed letter and the word Emma had delicately written on the Christmas tree. The unique curve of the letter "C" was unmistakable. Jane put her head back on the hard wood of the door and let out a low sigh of despair. It had been a young, frightened and angry young woman who had written those letters to the Colonel, but that did not make her an evil woman. She was a woman in pain. A young woman betrayed by a man she and her mother had trusted. The Colonel. Her father had turned his back on a woman he'd romanced and bedded. He had dismissed Emma's letters like so much garbage.

Who was the real monster?

Jane knew she had to turn over the Christmas tree cutout to Mr. Porter. He and Dr. Rydell had wanted proof. Well, she would give them their precious proof. Proof only that the Colonel had done the unforgivable. Her memory of her father suddenly lost its luster. He'd been only a man after all. The most despicable kind. Jane realized she could forgive Emma anything, but she could never forget what her father had done. To turn his back on his own unborn child was inconceivable.

She wished she could knock on Emma's door and let her know what was set to transpire below. Jane preferred to hear what Emma had to say, but she knew the two impatient men downstairs would not wait. She was forced to fetch Emma later, after they revealed all to Cole.

With her heart gripped by fear and anticipation, Jane ran downstairs to meet her two anxious visitors. She handed them the crumpled old letter and the paper cutout to Mr. Porter, who took it with a surprised expression.

"You wanted proof, gentlemen," Jane said in a low, constrained voice. "Emma made that paper cutout for Henry and wrote the words. It is the same handwriting."

The two men stared at it quietly, comparing it to the other letter. Dr. Rydell met Jane's eyes.

"There is no doubt then. It is as we suspected. We must speak with Cole immediately. Do you know where Miss Stiles might be tonight?"

Jane crossed her arms. "When I left here, she was in her room." She felt dirty sharing information about Emma with Dr. Rydell. She would not answer any further of his questions. "Cole is no doubt in the library—quite drunk by this time, I would guess." She dreaded the fury that would certainly erupt from her brother.

As the three of them approached the library, they saw the doors gaping open and the echoes of Emma's voice drifted through into the hallway.

"You haven't even the sense or courage to face me, you cowardly, whining wreck of a man. And to think someone like you could pass judgment on people like me, people better than you but not in your class."

In an agonizing voice, Cole said. "Go ahead, shoot me, you would be doing me a great service, I assure you. Yes, put me out of my misery. But if you are not going to fire that gun, then go away and leave me alone." His voice was slurred. Cole was drunk out of his mind.

"Get up off that chair and act like the son of the great and mighty Colonel Vincent Havens. Look at me and see me, unlike what your miserable father did to my mother. You are no better than your wicked father. Your Colonel ruined my mother on a mere whim...a lark of lust. Oh, he had his fun, didn't he? We welcomed him into our humble but poor little cabin. He taught me useless things like how to make rabbits out of napkins. Did he teach you that too, Cole?"

"Get out! You came here like a snake, with lies. You cloaked all your moves in the shadows, hiding behind my sister Jane's skirts."

"Quiet!" Emma screamed. "Your father rode away, leaving my mother pregnant. I wrote him countless letters pleading for help. I begged for my mother's life. She would not have died so miserably had your father acknowledged her or my letters and sent help. We would be sharing a little brother right now, possibly right here in Havenswood, if he had given all of us a chance. Instead, they are dead and I was left to find way alone in the ugly streets of New York. How would you have handled that, Cole? Answer me!"

"Well," Cole said, his voice broken. "What are you going to do with that poor excuse for a gun, shoot it or just point it at me?"

Jane could wait no longer. She rushed into the library, Dr. Rydell and Mr. Porter at her heels.

They walked into a scene that nearly cut Jane's heart in two. Cole sat slumped, his clothes in disarray and hair falling down his eyes, on the horsehair chair in front of the unlit fireplace. Emma stood only several feet away, pointing a small pocket pistol at him.

"Emma! No!" Jane called out.

Emma's eyes opened wide in shock and her mouth gaped in surprise. She turned the gun and pointed it directly at Jane. Cole struggled to get up but Jane stopped him by putting out her hand.

She stared directly at Emma.

"I choose to believe you will not harm me or anyone else with that, my darling. Why not hand it to me? Everything will be fine, I promise. Henry is safe and sound in bed upstairs."

Jane saw the immediate relief in Emma's face and the arm pointing the gun waivered.

"Please, Emma. Put the gun down. You have every right to be angry, and I know you want to seek revenge and get even, but all that is behind you now. You have

167

found me and I love you immensely." Jane walked toward her slowly. "Please, come to me now. Let me have the gun." She held out a hand toward Emma.

Dr. Rydell and Peter Porter stood frozen behind her.

She was only inches from Emma. She could see the tear stained cheeks and quivering lips of her beloved.

Emma gazed at her with tear filled eyes.

"Please forgive me, my Jane."

She suddenly lowered her arm and slowly handed the gun to Jane, who scooped her up in her arms and held her tight as Emma broke down in sobs.

Chapter 16

The library at Havenswood was now the setting for a strange scene. Henry was hopefully still sound asleep upstairs. The Brownes, awakened and startled by the screaming and commotion, had rang their bell wildly, but were calmed by a quick visit by Dr. Rydell.

Cole sat in his chair, dazed and stiff. He did not remove his gaze from Emma, who was seated with Jane beside her on the red velvet settee across from him. Dr. Rydell stood near Cole, his arm on the fireplace mantle. Peter Porter stood beside Jane and Emma. She remained quiet, her eyes cast down.

Mr. Porter leaned down and passed the locket to her.

"You vouch for the fact that this is your mother, Amanda Collins?"

Emma looked at the miniature, then back at Jane, who squeezed her hand and smiled.

"Yes, that was my mother." She replied quietly but boldly.

He nodded. "Well, it's easy to believe. But tell me something, Miss Stiles, now that your secret is out, I would be a fool to believe that you merely found me and my office by chance that day."

Emma shook her head slowly. "No, not by chance."

"How did you know about my advertisement in the newspapers?"

"It was easy. I worked for a time at the New York Times. It was fate that I was there when your ad came in. I made sure that it never ran in the paper at all. That is why you never got responses. It was easy to send you a proof that never saw the light of day. I decided the time was right to exact the vengeance I vowed to my dying mother. I promised myself that I would get even with Colonel Havens and his entire family. I fully intended to inflict as much pain on Cole Havens, Henry Havens and—" Her gaze traveled from Cole to Jane and stopped. She smiled a weak smile. "I fell in love with Jane Havens and I'm no longer ashamed to openly admit it."

"Why, I never—"

"Shut up, Cole," Jane said sharply, her eyes blazing in anger. "This is no longer about you and your inadequacies." She looked at Emma with loving eyes. "My darling, we won't need to hide anymore..." She paused, hesitant to ask the question that had been worrying her the most. "Emma, were you responsible for the horrid accidents? Please, you can be honest with me."

Emma's shoulders slouched forward and she dropped her head. Her voice was so low, Jane could barely hear her.

"I never wanted anyone to get hurt. I only wanted them to feel the pain and fear I felt. The anguish and hurt my mother suffered—" She turned and grabbed Jane by the shoulders. "Oh, dear Jane, you must believe me. I never lied to you once...once I fell in love with you. Everything I told you about my life and my mother was true. I never wanted Henry or the Brownes to be in danger for their lives. I've never really handled horses. I'd read where one could fool with a bridle and cause issues with command of the animal. I imagined the horses would

170

refuse to move. I never once thought they would run amok. I suffered dearly when I heard the horses had to be put to death, and the Brownes were seriously injured. And my gun was not loaded. I never intended to kill Cole or anyone."

"The gun is not loaded, she is telling the truth," Dr. Rydell added. "But Miss Stiles, your acts of villainy should not go unpunished. You conspired to cause harm, and Gabe and Hannah Browne were lucky to come away without more serious injuries. And if I hadn't happened by in the creek—"

"I never would have allowed Henry to drown," Emma spoke up. "I did not know he had gone so far in search of the egg to give me. I left him in the cave with Goldy, which I was convinced would bring Henry safely back home."

"I'm sorry, Miss Stiles," Mr. Porter said softly. "Yes, an injustice was done to your mother, and you suffered. There is no excuse for that. The Colonel was not a saint. But the fact still remains that you falsified your letters of reference. If I had not been blinded by your beauty like the old fool that I am, I should have questioned those documents before embracing you and bringing you here to Havenswood. Do you deny forging your references?"

Emma shook her head silently, eyes still downcast. Mr. Porter sighed and stuffed his hands into his pockets.

"That is against the law, Miss Stiles."

Jane suddenly got up, smiled down at Emma, and put out her hand for her.

"Emma, I'm going to ask you to wait in your room for me. Please? I shall be up as soon as Mr. Porter and I are finished."

Emma stood up, uncertainty and apprehension on her face. Jane took her hand.

"It's all right. I promise." She smiled, not feeling as sure as she portrayed, but she had to remain strong if she was to convince Cole and Mr. Porter of her plan. Left to her own devices, she would have kissed Emma, but she could not push her chances. She had already shamed Cole, and judging by the scowl on his face, and the looks of surprise on her guests' faces, she had also earned their disapproval and disgust.

As soon as Emma had left the room, Cole slammed his fist on the arm of the chair and got up.

"I knew there was something inhuman about her."

Jane whirled to face him.

"Of all the people to point fingers, Cole, you are the least entitled. Emma came here and transformed Henry into a true little gentleman. Something both of us failed miserably at."

"She toyed with us like a demon, that's what she did," Cole ranted. "She blinded us with her charm and magic, and then proceeded to try and destroy our family." He glared at Jane with the glassy eyes of alcohol.

"I love her, Cole. There are demons within us all, just as surely as there is the goodness of Christ. Love is blind to both." She looked from Cole to Dr. Rydell and Mr. Porter. "Emma risked her life to save Goldy. Did any of you forget that? There is goodness in her heart. None of you here would have lasted a night in her life. The scars she bears on her body are the sins of my father—" She gazed steadily at her brother. "Our father, Cole. Yes, our father used the match to start the fire of vengeance that burned a hole in Emma's soul. Instead of standing here passing judgment and calling for justice, we should be ashamed of ourselves instead. Ashamed for the sins of our father and the blind faith in him that clouded our lives."

There was a long silence in the room. Only the tick tock of the clock broke the heavy silence. Jane came to stand before Mr. Porter.

"Mr. Porter," she began softly. "Yes, Emma may have presented you with false papers of references, and I'm certain a part of your hurt is that your ego has been bruised, but you should have been more vigilant. She did you no harm." She paused and smiled at the old friend of the family. He lowered his head and looked away.

Jane looked at Dr. Rydell, who had not moved from the fireplace.

"Dr. Rydell, the only harm that has been done here is to the Havens family and to Hannah and Gabe Browne. I will not lift a finger to accuse Emma or demand justice—"

"Well, you do not sway me so easily, sister," Cole's eyes blazed. "She meant to kill us all."

"She did not," Jane said, returning the angry stare. "She may have wanted to when she wrote those letters, but the part of her heart that remains unscarred stopped her from doing us any real harm."

Mr. Porter had come up behind Jane and touched her arm softly. There was a smile in his eyes.

"Miss Jane, I can't pretend that I approve of any of this, but I reckon my practice nor I suffered any harm from Miss Stiles's deceptions..." He looked hard at her, searching her face. "Please reconsider your future, Miss Jane. Think of your brothers and Havenswood."

Jane knew what he meant. Get rid of Emma Stiles. Find yourself a nice young man and marry him.

Cole growled. "She cares nothing for Henry or me, only for that, that—"

"Stop it this instance!" Jane screamed. "It is exactly because I care about you and dear Henry more than anything in my heart that I could make the decision I've made."

Dr. Rydell cleared his throat.

"Look here, this has been a hell of a night and I'm certain Peter here is as tired as I am. I've got an early patient and I think you two need to have a family conversation...alone."

"Yes. Yes, I quite agree, my friend," Peter Porter agreed wearily. "This is something for Jane and Cole to discuss." He bowed to both Jane and Cole. "We shall be on our way, then."

"Goodnight, Cole, Miss Havens," Dr. Rydell said. He eyed Cole for a long moment. Cole never said a word. "You know where my office is, Cole. Come see me if you need to talk." Rydell walked out of the room.

Mr. Porter followed him but stopped at the doorway and looked back.

"I am so sorry the both of you had to hear about the Colonel and...and—"

"It's all right, Mr. Porter," Jane said. "We, as a family, owe you so much. And thank you for your kindness to Emma. You made the right decision."

He only looked at her and shook his head before walking out.

Cole nearly stumbled toward the bottle in the open cabinet. Jane blocked his way and took his shoulders.

"Not now, Cole. You're drunk already. I need you as sober as is possible. We need to talk."

He shrugged her off with one violent push, his eyes moist.

"I won't speak with you, Jane. You've had a hand in destroying our family." He pointed to the doorway. "You've...you've sheltered and committed who knows what unspeakable acts with...her."

"What I've done is none of your business, and none of Mr. Porter's nor Dr. Rydell's business either."

She moved closer to her brother. She could not plan her future as long as the venom of hate between them lingered behind.

"Cole," she said quietly, calmly. "I love you and Henry more than my own life—"

"You could have fooled me."

"Listen to me, please. I'm leaving Havenswood, Cole. But I don't want to leave like this. I need your blessing, and peace between us."

Cole stared at her, mouth open in shock.

Jane smiled. "Yes, I'm leaving. Emma and I will go to New York, Boston, Philadelphia, anywhere where she can find employment. I shall need to find something to do as well. I know it won't be easy, being unmarried women, but it must be our future. I will ask Mr. Porter for a letter of recommendation. He most likely will be delighted to supply both Emma and myself with anything just to see us both away from Havens Falls."

Cole ran a hand through his hair, let out a cry of despair, and sank into the chair. Sobs wracked his body.

"Why, Jane? Why must you leave and ruin our lives?" He looked up at her. "I don't want to see you go. What will become of Henry...me? I need—"

"Yes, I know you need me, even though you never spared me from your belittling comments. But I think I may be more of a crutch for you now. Maybe you'll learn to grow up and not put so much responsibility on me. It's time for you to step up and give me and the Brownes a break."

She went down on her knees beside him and took his hands. He squeezed her fingers tightly.

"Jane, why did father have to ruin our memories? Why? This whole place, it feels tainted."

"Cole, don't you see? This is an opportunity for the both of us. We can both make a fresh start. Make Havenswood yours. Work the land. The crops will be good this year, we can all feel it. Create your own, new memories to fill this house with. Get married. Start your own family. And take good care of Henry. He will grow into a big, strong young man."

He managed a small smile. "Must you go, sister?"

Jane nodded and smiled warmly. "Yes, but I need you to promise me that you will forgive Emma and not hold her into account. Cole, you, of all of us, know what demons we meet at the end of our rope."

He only stared at her, holding fast to her hands. In his eyes, Jane saw that Cole understood. Yes, he had faced those same demons.

She got up, letting go of her brother.

"I've much to do tomorrow. Henry will be foremost on my mind. I shall go to Havens Falls and speak with Mr. Porter."

Cole leaned his back into the chair. "I won't know what to do without you."

Jane couldn't cry. She could not break down now. What Cole needed was her strength, not her tears. Cole and Henry had Havenswood. They had each other to love. Emma had no one, until now. Jane was convinced she was doing the right thing and she knew she had convinced Cole of that as well.

"Brother, what you need right now is to get to bed and find some sleep. And then clear out that cabinet of the alcohol first thing in the morning."

She bent down, kissed the top of his tousled hair, and walked out of the library, leaving the doors open. Nothing would ever be the same again.

Chapter 17

Jane thought her heart would burst as she practically ran up the main stairs, nearly tripping on her skirt and made her way to Emma's room. But first, she stopped in front of Henry's door and pulled it open gently, to find her little brother fast asleep and snoring lightly. She wiped a tear from her eye and walked out as quietly as she'd entered.

Jane took a deep breath. She felt conflicted and apprehensive as she knocked lightly on Emma's door.

"Emma, it's Jane."

It took a few moments for the door to open and Jane halted at the doorframe, horrified at the sight that greeted her. Emma stood, her eyes red from crying. Her blue nightgown was stained with streaks of blood.

"Dear God!" Jane rushed to her and embraced her tightly. "What have you done, my darling? What have you done?" She looked toward the bed and saw the small tree branch, its stark, long narrow twigs tinged with blood.

Emma covered her face with her hands. "I could not bear the wickedness I committed against you and your family." She looked at Jane with despair in her blue eyes. "It is the only way I know to atone for my own sins."

Jane took the tree branch, violently broke it in half, and flung it into the fireplace.

"We'll start a fire and burn that thing, forever, my love. You never need to punish yourself, not by switch nor any other way."

She gently removed the bloodied gown from Emma's body. She stood fully naked before Jane. It broke Jane's heart to see the small, bleeding welts along Emma's back, shoulders and arms.

"Oh, my darling, I will wipe away these scars. I shall kiss them and make them disappear forever."

She took one of the fresh towels from the dresser and began to wipe down the wounds gently, kissing each new mark with tenderness. The taste of blood lingered on her tongue.

"We are leaving, my Emma. Together, we will make a new life away from Havenswood."

"No," Emma murmured, "this is your home, it is I—"

Jane stopped her with a finger to her lips.

"Shh." She continued to clean up Emma's arms. "I give you my heart, my soul, my life. Will that be enough to save you from your nightmares? I can't promise, my love, but let me try." She gazed deeply into the icy blue of Emma's tear-stained eyes. She saw only a helpless woman, not a vengeful soul. "We can do this. It may not be a lavish existence, but it will be ours alone. Trust me, love."

Emma smiled. "Don't you know, dear Jane? You saved me the minute I fell in love with you."

Jane placed the bloodied nightgown and towel on the wingback chair and grabbed Emma by the hand, leading her to the bed.

"I won't be leaving your bed tonight, darling. We no longer need to hide in Havenswood."

She leaned in and pressed her lips softly on Emma's lips. Emma responded hungrily, holding Jane tightly, her tongue dipping into Jane's mouth.

They fell onto the bed, Emma lying softly atop Jane, covering her body with her hungry kisses, Jane's fingers deep into Emma's black tresses. For a while they caressed one another gently, slowly.

"Have you no doubts about me, Jane...no lingering questions? I would not begrudge you if you did."

"No darling, I believe you. I believe you meant only to duplicate in us the fear and terror you felt when your mother was so ill. I can only imagine how alone you must have felt, the losses that shattered your trust. How you suffered. But I could never imagine you wishing us real harm. I am here to help you heal the wounds that brought this on, darling...if you will let me...if you will trust me."

Emma looked into Jane's eyes and without intention, without plan, without restraint, her tears fell onto Jane's face in a hot stream of regret and sadness.

"Is it not too late for me, dear Jane? I know you love me, and you must surely know how I love you, but has my soul gone too far to be reclaimed? You must tell me, Jane, you must!"

Jane smudged the tears aside with her finger. She held Emma's head in her hands and pulled her close. She spoke to her slowly, deliberately. She couldn't have said, later, the exact words she spoke. She didn't know anyone who could ever move her to make proclamations she was whispering to Emma. But when she saw the slow smile spreading across her beautiful face, Jane knew she had said the right things.

Emma began to kiss and caress Jane, tracing her fingers and her tongue down her body. Jane let out a moan of ecstasy as Emma's moist tongue reached between her open, waiting legs.

"Oh, Emma, I am on fire for you. Make love to me tonight, all night."

As their love making intensified, the candles in the room burned hotter and the shadows upon the walls danced to the rhythm of the ecstasy on the bed.

Chapter 18

*S*pread out on the porch at Havenswood sat several large suitcases, a small trunk and one small bag. They contained the entire belongings of Jane Havens.

Out back, in the Havenswood garden, summer had sprung and the air was alive with the colors and scents of the season. A warm breeze blew through the blooming wisteria, sending the colorful flowers floating through the air.

Jane stood beneath the giant tree, a big smile upon her lips. Reliving the memory of her first night of lovemaking with Emma would always bring a smile.

She waited for a coach to take her to the train station where Emma waited. Emma had already moved to the Wilkins House while Jane tied up loose ends and said her goodbyes to Havenswood—her childhood home and the land of her parents and forefathers. Jane couldn't help but feel a tinge of regret and shame overcame her as she thought about her father. But her thoughts were interrupted by her brother, Cole, who had walked up behind her. He carried her hat. He fidgeted as he watched her with saddened eyes.

She could see his pain but there was something else there behind his eyes of goodbye. There was renewed determination. She smiled as she shielded the sun from her eyes.

"Well," he said, "the coach should be here any moment..." He paused and held up her hat. "I thought you might need this."

"Cole, please take care of the wisteria and the garden." Jane took her hat and pinned it securely atop her auburn curls. "This is right for the both us, you know—"

"But Havenswood—"

"Havenswood is no longer my home. I will never again feel happy here, knowing what my father did before he returned here. Make it yours, Cole. Bring it back to life. Paint beautiful pictures and write poetry. Marry a special lady who is worthy of your love and attentions, and this house, then bring new blood to the Havens name. It's time."

"But Henry—"

"Henry took the news quite well," Jane said. "I told him that once Emma and I are settled, he can come and visit for special holidays. Cole, you may be too stubborn to admit it, but he learned so much from Emma. He will grow to be a fine young gentleman and I'm sure he will make the Havens name proud once again." Her face turned somber. "I expect you to clean yourself up, brother. Henry needs a whole man to bring him up the way a big brother should be a role model to his younger sibling. If I get news that...Henry is not happy, I will not hesitate to remove him from Havenswood and have him live with us." She searched his eyes.

"You needn't worry. I expect Henry will be a big part of putting this old house back to shape again. We shall do it together. And you, Jane? What about you?"

"I have everything I prayed for. I know most would condemn me and think I have lost my soul, but I know in my heart that I have not. What can be more precious than to find true love?"

She put out a hand to him and smiled. "Never mind, you needn't answer that, Cole."

He looked away, shifted his feet, and then looked at her as he took her hand.

"You are my sister. Nothing and no one will ever get in the way of my love for you..." He paused, put a hand on his hips and looked down at the ground. "But please forgive me, sister, I cannot accept that..."

"Her name is Emma and she and I are as one. I love her. How can you say you love me yet not her, when she makes me so happy?"

"I do not have your gentle soul, Jane," Cole despaired. "Maybe, perhaps, in time...I hope you will forgive me."

Jane shook her head. "There is nothing to forgive, brother. I continue to pray that God gives you strength with your own demons and that you don't allow the drink to destroy you. You have Henry to care for now. And Havenswood."

She swept her brother into her arms for a tight embrace and then broke free. The sound of the rolling and squeaking wheels of a heavy carriage reached her ears.

"It's time, Cole. Don't worry about me. Mr. Porter was kind enough to advance me a loan on a third of the worth of Havenswood, payable when I get employment. But this is more than enough. I will send you both my new address, wherever that may be."

Cole smiled but not a happy smile. "We are family. You shall not disappear from our lives that easily...my sister."

Jane let go of his hand and pulled away, finally turning her back and walking toward the front porch where her luggage waited.

"Janey! Janey!" Henry was running toward her. He flung himself into her arms and held on to her waist tightly. "I wanted to see you before you left."

Jane ruffled his hair and was pained to see the tears in his eyes. She swallowed the lump in her throat.

"Now, you're a grown young gentleman, Henry. Cole is going to need all your help. And you'll look after him for me, right? Like we talked about?"

He nodded, wiping his eyes. "You still have to go, right?"

Jane took a deep breath and exhaled. "Yes, Henry, I do. But you'll be visiting as soon as Emma and I get settled. We'll have lovely times."

She knew if she stayed any longer, parting was going to be more painful than she ever imagined. And the pain in her heart bit just as if a knife had plunged into it, for she knew the life Emma and she faced would be fraught with uncertainties and perhaps even poverty. It would not be the proper place for Henry.

She held her little brother's shoulders. "You write if you need to, Henry. If things don't go right with your brother, you get Mr. Porter to write me. Remember to always be a proper gentleman. Now, go check on Cole. I left him under the big wisteria in the garden."

He looked at her, a sad little smile on his face and lingered for only a few seconds before he planted a soft kiss on her cheek and took off running toward the garden.

Jane could not bear to look after him. She could not break down now. Instead, she took one last, lingering look at Havenswood, her thoughts pensive yet hopeful. She struggled to control the sadness that was gathering within.

She finally began to cry as she entered the carriage and the driver closed the door. He loaded her baggage on top of the roof quickly. Jane found that her tears tasted of joy mingled with the sadness of goodbye. She took no regrets with her.

As the carriage pulled away, Jane could barely see Cole and Henry standing beneath the beautiful purple tree.

"Goodbye, Havenswood. Take good care of them all."

Patty G. Henderson is an author, artist and publisher. She loves history and historical literature, film and television. She's also a fan of supernatural literature and films, and the author of the Brenda Strange Supernatural Mystery series as well as three Gothic Historical Romances and several anthologies.

"My passion to write comes from a desire to entertain. Nothing more. I come from a family who loved to tell tales around the dinner table, my grandmother fondest of ghost stories. If I've managed to lure a reader into another place and time, and after they close the book, the story still lingers, then I've done what I love doing as a writer."

"If I succeeded in doing that, I would be very grateful if you took a few minutes to write a review on Amazon for PASSION FOR VENGEANCE or any of my books that you should happen across. Reviews can be very helpful, and I absolutely love to read the various insights from satisfied readers. Thank you so very much. Until we meet again..."

Patty's Gothic Historical Romances

The Secret of Lighthouse Pointe
Castle of Dark Shadows
Passion for Vengeance

Patty's Brenda Strange Supernatual Series

The Burning of Her Sin
Tangled and Dark
The Missing Page
Ximora

All books are available as eBooks and Trade Paperbacks on Amazon and Barnes and Noble.

Please visit me at my web site:
www.pattyghenderson.com

www.ingramcontent.com/pod-product-compliance
Lightning Source LLC
Chambersburg PA
CBHW020118180626
46812CB00006B/2642